'Which side of the bed do you want?'

The one you're on.

Nope, she couldn't say that. She was going for cool and sophisticated. 'Whatever.'

Brilliant! She sounded as if sharing a bed with a man she barely knew was something she'd done so many times before.

'I usually sleep on the left,' he said.

Ouch. She'd let herself forget that this was a man who was used to sharing his bed. With lots of different women. And if he gave them come-to-bed looks like the one he was giving her right now, it was hardly surprising.

'Whatever,' she said again, faking nonchalance.

Concentrating on every step, she walked over to the bed. The one thing she couldn't do was to drop her towel in front of him. She couldn't get into bed wearing the towel, either.

'Would you mind turning away?' she said.

'Sure.'

To her relief, Max did the gentlemanly thing. Just in case he *was* tempted to peek, she turned her back. And dropped the towel…

Kate Hardy lives on the outskirts of Norwich with her husband, two small children, a dog—and too many books to count! She wrote her first book at the age of six, when her parents gave her a typewriter for her birthday. She had the first of a series of sexy romances published when she was twenty-five, and swapped a job in marketing communications for freelance health journalism when her son was born so she could spend more time with him. She's wanted to write for Mills & Boon® since she was twelve—and when she was pregnant with her daughter, her husband pointed out that writing Medical Romances™ would be the perfect way to combine her interest in health issues with her love of good stories. Now Kate has ventured into Modern Romance™, and *The Cinderella Project* is her first novel for this series.

Kate is always delighted to hear from readers—do drop in to her website at www.katehardy.com

Look out for **Her Honourable Playboy**—
Kate Hardy's latest Medical Romance™—
also available this month, wherever
Mills & Boon® books are sold.

THE CINDERELLA PROJECT

BY
KATE HARDY

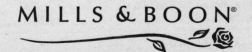

MILLS & BOON®

All the characters in this book have no existence outside the imagination of the author, and have no relation whatsoever to anyone bearing the same name or names. They are not even distantly inspired by any individual known or unknown to the author, and all the incidents are pure invention.

First published in Great Britain 2006
Harlequin Mills & Boon Limited,
Eton House, 18-24 Paradise Road, Richmond, Surrey TW9 1SR

© Pamela Brooks 2006

ISBN 0 263 84987 2

Set in Times Roman 10½ on 11½ pt.
171-0406-59622

Printed and bound in Spain
by Litografia Rosés S.A., Barcelona

For Gerard, who still makes my knees go weak—
with all my love

CHAPTER ONE

'ALL right. 'Fess up. Just tell me what you've done.' Max Taylor looked suspiciously at his PA.

'Nothing.'

Lisa looked the picture of innocence. Five feet ten, slender, pretty, with long blonde hair cut in the latest fashionable style. But Max knew his PA was more than just a clothes-horse for the designer gear she favoured. She was an organisational demon who could charm the hardest heart. When she had that kind of smile on her face, it meant she was plotting something.

'You brought me my favourite coffee first thing this morning.'

'I always do.'

'And chocolate biscuits. The really *nice* kind.'

'Because you deserve a treat, sweet cheeks.'

Fear lurched in his stomach. Was this a goodbye treat? He forced himself to sound light-hearted. 'Please don't tell me you've been offered a his 'n' hers film contract and you're going back to Hollywood with Joe.'

She laughed. 'No. He's got another month to go on this contract, and anyway if I went back to acting I'd rather be in theatre. Treading the boards is way better—you actually see your audience. With film, you just have a crew and the extras and amazingly hot lights and a cold, cold camera lens. And you don't get audience reaction from a camera.'

'You've been offered a dream job, one you can't refuse, and you're going to start it tomorrow?'

'I already have a dream job.' Lisa batted her eyelashes at him, then blew him a kiss. 'And a dream boss.'

'Okay, now I'm really worried. You normally spend most of the morning insulting me. Today, you've been all sweetness and light.'

'There's nothing to worry about. Hey, I know I'm not going to move you from that desk until you've tweaked those plans, so I brought you some lunch. Smoked salmon bagel. Oh, and some fresh strawberries.'

His favourites. And it was March, so the strawberries were out of season. She was definitely up to something. 'Are you going to tell me, or do I have to threaten to fire you?'

'Okay.' She spread her hands, looking all innocence. 'I need a favour.'

He exhaled. Very, very slowly. He'd heard that before, so he knew what it meant. Business as usual. He wasn't about to lose the best PA he'd ever had and go through the headache of finding a replacement, then the inevitable settling-in period while they got used to the way each other worked. 'Don't tell me. There was a pair of shoes yelling your name, your credit card's up to its limit and you need an advance on your salary or some overtime, right now. All right. Whatever. It's fine by me.' He waved a dismissive hand. Problem sorted. Now he could get back to work.

'Actually, no. It's kind of…personal.'

Now she had his attention. She wasn't coming on to him, was she? He liked Lisa—he liked her a lot—but she wasn't his type. And she was already engaged, to an actor. Joe was filming away on location most of the time, so the relationship tended to be long distance, but Max was sure he'd seen her flicking through a stack of bridal magazines recently…hadn't he? Besides, he didn't do serious relationships. Not since Gina. Right now, he was focused on his career—on bringing neglected houses back to life and winning awards for his work. Which meant he didn't have time to lavish attention on a serious girlfriend. And if Lisa had split up with Joe, he definitely wasn't going to be her 'transition' romance. No way was he going to exchange a brilliant working relationship for one night of good sex. For one night of wonderful sex, even. Lisa was in the pigeon-hole marked 'colleague' and she was staying there.

'How do you mean, *personal*?' he asked suspiciously.

'I have this friend. She has to go to the wedding from hell, and she needs a partner to go with her.'

'So how does that involve me?'

'Well, duh.'

Max couldn't help laughing at the look on Lisa's face when she realised what she'd said and tried to backtrack fast. 'Oh, no. I was going to play this sweet. I was going to be so *nice* to you.'

'I knew it couldn't last. You want me to be her date for the day?' He shook his head. 'Sorry, Lise. It sounds like a bad idea.'

'No strings. You never, ever have to see each other again after this one day.'

'It's very sweet of you to try and fix me up, but I'm not looking for Ms Right.' He was perfectly happy with Ms Right Now—someone who knew the rules: that a date was for fun, and having sex didn't mean that he was desperate to put a platinum band on the ring finger of her left hand.

'I'm not fixing you up,' Lisa protested. 'It's…escort duty. A favour to me, as your best-ever PA.'

Max raised an eyebrow. 'You want me to go to a wedding with a girl I don't even know.'

'She's lovely,' Lisa said.

'If she's so lovely,' Max asked, 'how come she doesn't have a date already?'

'Because...' Lisa growled in frustration. 'Look, she's like you. She loves her job more than anything else, so she doesn't date.'

Okay, he'd concede the point on the job front. But he dated. Just not the same woman more than three times. 'Hasn't she got any male friends she can ask? Someone she works with?'

Lisa scoffed. 'Hardly. She works in IT. This is a flash wedding, so she needs someone who can wear a suit without looking like a schoolboy who's been forced into it to please his mother. I would've lent her Joe for the day, but you know he's on location. He can't get the time off. And anyway, you look fabulous in a suit.'

The suit he wore to planning meetings and client meetings. On site, he was more likely to wear jeans and a hard hat. Brick dust didn't go well with Italian designer suits. 'Sorry. Count me out.'

'You never know, you might even enjoy it,' she wheedled.

'Yeah, and I might enjoy having all my teeth extracted without any Novocaine. Weddings aren't my thing, Lisa.'

'Then pretend it's not a wedding. Pretend you're schmoozing a client.'

He folded his arms. 'I don't schmooze.' He didn't need to, because he already had the best advertising: word of mouth from satisfied clients whose houses he'd restored. To the point where he had a waiting list.

She lifted her hands in surrender. 'I take it back. Wrong word. I meant *charm*. All you have to do is smile and be nice. You can do that.'

He sighed. 'Lise, I don't have time for this. I have work to do. Like now.'

'One day, that's all I'm asking.'

'No.'

'It's this Saturday. And I know there's nothing in your diary. Please?' At his silence, she added, 'I'll work overtime. For free. I won't make any personal calls for a whole month.'

Max, who'd been about to point out that she had yet to earn her salary today, let alone overtime, was disarmed into laughing. 'Now *that* I'd pay to see.'

She brightened. 'Then that's my price. All you have to do is drive my friend to the wedding, stick by her side while you're there, and you'll be home by midnight.'

'You make her sound like Cinderella.'

'I wouldn't ask you if it wasn't important.' Lisa did the thing with her eyes that really annoyed him—it made her look like a cute little puppy-dog nobody could say no to, and even he wasn't completely immune. 'Cyn means a lot to me.'

'Cyn?' He did a double take. 'You mean her name actually *is* Cinderella?'

'No.' Lisa flapped her hand impatiently at him. 'It's Cynthia.'

Not a particularly modern name. According to Lisa, Cynthia didn't date, and she was a workaholic IT specialist. Max had a nasty feeling he knew the type. Mousy, no make-up and terrible clothes. Clever, but no social skills whatsoever. So Lisa wanted him to spend the whole of Saturday at a wedding where he wouldn't know anyone— as the escort of a woman who'd probably say no more than half a dozen words to him and really wanted to be back hiding behind her computer screen? He could think of quite a few things he'd much rather be doing. 'I'm sorry. You'll have to find someone else. I know Joe's away, but you know loads of people in showbiz. People who would be far more suitable than I would at playing Trophy Boy-friend for the day.'

'Think about it, Max. Please.'

Then again, his PA could nag for two continents, and he didn't have time for that right now. 'Okay, I'll think about it,' he said, just to shut her up. Except when she asked him again at the end of the day—as he just knew she would—the answer would still be no.

Later that afternoon, Max was taking a break from the plans he was working on and flicking through one of the trade journals. He'd just turned the fifth page in succession when he backtracked.

He recognised that house.

And he recognised that design.

But he hadn't got the tender. Someone else had. He'd been disappointed, because the house had reminded him of the first neglected building he'd fallen in love with and he'd really wanted to work on it. Then he also remembered the reason why he hadn't got the job: the client had chosen to go with another architect's designs.

Frowning, he left the magazine open on his desk and flicked into his computer. His archive files were properly indexed, so it was easy to dig out his original plans. And, yes, they matched the photographs of the restored house. Pretty much how he'd imagined the place to look when he'd submitted his tender.

Odd. Was his memory playing tricks?

He buzzed through to Lisa.

'Ah, you've changed your mind,' she said chirpily. 'I knew you'd see sense if I went on strike and refused to bring you coffee.'

He hadn't noticed, actually. 'Lise, do you remember Phil Watkins?'

'Forty pounds overweight, shiny suit, and the most terrible taste in ties?'

Trust her to remember the fashion details. 'That's the one. Can I have the file, please?'

'Sure. What's up?'

He wasn't ready to share his suspicions yet, even though he knew his PA was completely trustworthy. 'I just need to review the file.'

'I'll get it.'

Reviewing the file didn't make Max any happier, because his memory had been spot on. Phil Watkins' letter said he loved Max's designs but had decided to go with another architect's treatment.

Except, from the photographs in this magazine, the restoration team had worked from plans very, very similar to the ones Max had submitted. There were a few differences in the detail, but basically it was Max's vision.

Which left three possibilities.

One, Phil Watkins had cheated him—he'd said he was using a different architect but had gone ahead and used Max's work anyway. Unlikely, because he would have known that Max would find out when the work had been done—especially if the house was showcased in one of the period living magazines—and that would leave Watkins wide open to a damages claim through the courts.

Two, someone had copied Max's design, changed just enough to make it his own design, and undercut Max's quote. Unlikely, because Max worked for himself and only he and Lisa had access to his files. He hadn't given the file to anyone else, and Lisa definitely wouldn't steal from him, or sell him out, not even for a whole room of shoes. Max knew he was a good judge of character, and Lisa was absolutely sound.

Three, it was coincidence—some other architect had

looked round the building and seen exactly the same things that Max had. Well, that was possible, because he'd known it to happen before. Great minds thought alike, and all that. And when he looked at the photographs again, he could see a few differences. Not many, but enough maybe for this to be coincidence.

Still faintly uneasy, Max closed the file and turned back to his plans. He just about managed to grunt an acknowledgement to Lisa when she brought in a cup of coffee later that afternoon, and clearly she realised she wouldn't have his attention because she didn't bother nagging him about the wedding invitation before she left for the evening.

He didn't have much of a respite, though. The following evening, when he was driving Lisa home after a late business meeting, she brought up the subject again.

'You've had ages to think about it.'

'And the answer is still no.'

Lisa sighed. 'Look, I promise you, it's not a set-up. You're not Cyn's type, anyway.'

Max slanted her a glance. 'So what's wrong with me?'

'Nothing. You're perfect.'

He grinned. 'Liar.'

'If I give you the list of your faults, you'll definitely say no. So let's just say that you're perfect.' She drummed her fingers on her knee. 'Look, Max, I wouldn't ask you if I wasn't desperate.'

'So I'm the last resort, now?'

'Yes—no—oh, stop trying to be clever about this!' She gritted her teeth. 'Look, supposing you'd been the school swot and a gang of kids had made your life a misery. Wouldn't you want to turn up at the ringleader's wedding looking super-successful?'

Max decided not to point out that he *was* successful. 'I wasn't bullied at school.'

'But say you had been.'

He shrugged. 'Why go to the wedding in the first place? There's a small word. Two letters. Starts with N and ends in O.'

'Your favourite, you mean. Supposing there's a very good reason why she has to go?'

'Then it's her choice.'

'She can't get out of it. And she needs help. And…' Lisa growled in frustration. 'Look, I owe her. I'd been in London for a fortnight when the play I was in went belly-up. So I got a temp job while I was waiting for another director to take me on…and, two days into my temp job, my flat-share went belly-up, too. I'd fallen in love with London and I wanted to stay, but I was in a mess. Cyn worked in the department where I was temping and she offered me her spare room. And she hasn't ever kicked me out. She puts up with my shoe habit, she listens to me talking about meringue dresses—even though she hates them—and she's even agreed to wear one on my wedding day. She's my best friend, Max. I want to help her.'

'As I said the other day, ask one of your actor buddies to do it.'

Lisa rolled her eyes. 'I've already asked. They're busy. And they wouldn't be as good at it as you are. You're the real thing.'

'Flattery's going to get you nowhere.'

'Seriously. Cyn comes from a small village. She's good at her job—*really* good. She's always being head-hunted. She's got a first-class degree from Cambridge University. She's probably earning more than any of them. But they won't see that.' Lisa threw her hands into the air in exasperation. 'They'll just see that she isn't married yet and she's on the shelf at twenty-seven. The rest of them are going to turn up with their merchant banker husbands and double-barrelled surnames and two beautiful children. She's going to be the odd one out, unless she takes serious arm-candy with her.'

'Arm-candy.' Max pulled a face. 'What a vile expression.'

'Okay, TDH, then. Tall, dark, handsome—and successful. You're *perfect*. Be her Prince Charming for the evening,' Lisa urged. 'And don't worry, she's not going to think it means you want a serious relationship with her. You don't have a hope in hell of getting past her defences anyway.'

'Defences?'

'Uh, I shouldn't have said that.' Lisa wriggled in her seat, looking embarrassed. 'Ignore that. All you need to know is that you're safe. She's not looking for a relationship. Just someone who can fake it for one day. Don't say no just yet. Think about it.'

He'd already said no. He'd already thought about it. Nothing was going to change there. But he made a noise he hoped would satisfy her and make her change the subject.

When he parked outside her home, she turned to him with a smile. 'Want to come in for a coffee?'

Uh-oh. He knew that look on her face. She was plotting. 'And meet your friend, you mean?'

'No,' she said, surprising him. 'Cyn won't be home yet. She works later hours than you do.'

'Right.'

'I have cake,' Lisa added. 'Walnut cake.'

She knew he loved cake. Well, bribery wasn't going to work. He still wasn't going to take her friend to the wedding. 'You can bring me a slice tomorrow.'

'Apple for the teacher, cake for the boss?' She shook her head. 'You want cake, then you come in for a coffee.'

'No nagging,' Max warned.

She sighed. 'You're a hard man. Okay. No nagging.'

Though when she unlocked the front door, Max could hear music. A slushy pop ballad. Just the kind of music he hated. And, as far as Max knew, Lisa shared the house with only one person. Which meant that Cyn was home.

'I thought you said she wouldn't be here?' he said.

'I didn't think she would be.' There was genuine surprise on his PA's face; clearly she meant it. 'Look, you can go if you want.'

And be chicken? No, he'd meet Cyn. And he'd tell her 'no' to her face. Nicely—Max didn't believe in trampling on people's feelings—but firmly. 'You promised me cake. And you know my rule: underpromise and overdeliver.'

'In other words, you want a *big* bit of cake.'

'Got it in one.'

When they went into the kitchen, a woman was sitting at the table in front of a laptop. Cyn. Though it was impossible to see what she looked like—she was wrapped in a huge fluffy dressing gown, her hair was swathed in a towel, and she was wearing a face-pack. The only thing he could tell about her was that she had brown eyes. Huge brown eyes. Beautiful brown eyes.

Lisa's words echoed in his head. *She's going to be the odd one out, unless she takes serious arm-candy with her.* Max had never felt out of place—but his best friend from school had, once. Gavin had been the new boy, the one everyone teased and was horrible to. And Max, sick of the pettiness, had walked right up to Gavin and offered him half the bar of chocolate he'd bought that morning. Stopped the bullying in its tracks.

Who was going to do that for Cyn?

'Max, Cyn—Cyn, Max,' Lisa said economically.

Well, he knew who Cyn was. She probably knew who he was, too.

'Hello, Max.' The face-pack masked her expression, but her eyes said it all for her. She was squirming. 'Nice to meet you.' Cyn raised her teaspoon briefly in acknowl-edgement and put the lid on the tub of premium ice cream next to her.

Premium *coffee* ice cream, he noticed. His favourite. So they had one thing in common.

'Comfort eating?' Lisa asked.

Cyn shook her head. 'No. Thinking.'

Lisa scoffed. 'Yeah, and it looks like it from here. You're playing Wordbug, aren't you?'

'I'm thinking at the same time.' Cyn turned off the CD she was playing, flicked out of the game and closed her laptop. 'I'll leave you to it. Goodnight.'

Talk about blunt. This woman wouldn't even know how to begin to schmooze. Just as he'd thought. Techie—with no social skills. Though on the other hand she might just be embarrassed because he'd seen her looking as if she were in the middle of a spa day. 'You don't have to go on my account,' Max said politely. After all, this was *her* kitchen—he didn't want to push her out of it.

'No worries. I'm sure you two need to talk shop—and I have some letters to write, anyway.'

Her smile—what he could see of it—was shy but sweet. Guilt immediately started sawing at Max's conscience. She might have sounded a bit abrupt, but she was a nice woman. Just as Lisa had said. Genuine. She was in a mess and needed help. What was a single day out of his life? And it wasn't as if he'd had anything planned at the weekend. Just some chilling out—maybe a drive out to look at the site he was working on next, a workout in the gym, going out with his best friend for a couple of beers, if Gavin wasn't already doing something with his wife and kids. Nothing arranged. Nothing he couldn't change.

And when he looked at Cyn, he didn't see a predator, a woman who planned to trap him into a relationship and who wouldn't take no for an answer. She probably didn't even know Lisa had asked him to go to the wedding with her. She'd probably die of embarrassment if she knew. Though she was going to *have* to know, if he agreed to escort her.

'Would one of those letters be an invitation acceptance?' Max asked.

Cyn's eyes widened. 'How do you know about that?' Then she glared at Lisa. 'I really hope you didn't do what I think you did. You said you'd ask one of your actor mates.'

'I did. They were busy.' Lisa did her spaniel-eyed look, but clearly Cyn was used to it because she ignored it.

'I apologise for my best friend. She shouldn't have imposed on you,' Cyn said to Max. 'Just ignore whatever she said.'

'So it's not the wedding from hell?' he asked.

'Unfortunately, it is.' She shrugged. 'But I'll deal with it.'

Brave words. But he caught that tiny look in her eyes. As if she were about to be flung to a pack of howling, slavering wolves.

Ah, hell. That lame duck habit had landed him with Gina in the first place. An unholy mess that had taken too much time and too much pain to sort out. He knew better than to get involved.

But his mouth had already made the decision for him. 'What time do you want me to pick you up on Saturday?'

CHAPTER TWO

'I CAN'T believe you did that.' Cyn paced up and down the kitchen, an hour later, dressed in jeans and a T-shirt and minus the face-pack. 'He's your *boss*!'

'I know, and he's perfect for Trophy Boyfriend,' Lisa said with a smile. 'He's exactly what you described to me. Rich, successful, clever—and all your old classmates will be green with envy that you've landed someone so gorgeous. He'll charm their mums. And you can have a ball on Saturday night, Cyn-derella.'

'Not funny.' Cyn continued to pace. 'He's taking me to this wedding out of *pity*.'

'You're the one who said you needed either a body double or a trophy boyfriend,' Lisa pointed out. 'There weren't any body doubles available. So I got you the trophy.'

Exactly what Cyn needed. She didn't want to upstage the bride; she just wanted to prove that the girl with no dad was just as good as the girl who could trace her family tree back a couple of centuries on both sides.

'And I'll make you the sexiest woman on the planet into the bargain,' Lisa promised. 'Marilyn Monroe with extra diamonds and glitter.'

Cyn scowled. 'I don't have the same colouring as

Marilyn Monroe. I hate glitz. I'm not bleaching my hair platinum-blonde and wearing a white dress and standing over an air vent!'

'Figure of speech.' Lisa flapped her hand dismissively. 'What I mean is, I'll make you look fabulous. Like Elizabeth Taylor, then—you've got her colouring.'

'No, I haven't. I've got brown eyes. And if you dollop make-up all over me, I'll look like a clown.' Cyn shook her head. 'N—O. No. Absolutely not,' she added, just in case Lisa hadn't got the message.

'You won't look like a clown,' Lisa soothed. 'Just give me a free hand.'

'A free hand? Why does that phrase worry me?' Cyn asked.

'Because you're chicken.' Lisa stuck out her tongue. 'Bottom line, Cyn, you saved my bacon when I needed a friend. Now it's my turn to do the same for you.' She took a swig of coffee. 'So I'm going to be your fairy godmother. We'll get your hair done on Friday night—I'll refresh it Saturday morning, and do your make-up. Nothing over the top, I promise—I'll keep it low key. You'd be surprised what a few lowlights, a tiny bit of foundation, mascara and lipstick can do. And we're going to go shopping tomorrow night and get you something to wear. Ooh, and new shoes. *Pretty* shoes.'

Cyn groaned. 'You're going to bankrupt me.'

Lisa grinned back. 'You might want to work some overtime before your credit-card bill comes in. You'll look a million dollars by the time I've finished.' At Cyn's raised eyebrow, she added, 'It won't cost you *quite* that much.'

'I'm less worried about that than I am about Prince Charming.'

'There's nothing to worry about. Max will be a perfect

gentleman. You're not each other's type, anyway. He works hard and plays harder, and you just work hard and work harder.'

Cyn bit her lip. 'I just hope he doesn't think that going to a wedding with me will give me stupid ideas. Can you make sure he knows I'm not looking for a rich husband— or even a poor one?'

'I know, I know.' Lisa rolled her eyes. 'You're too busy with your career to settle down with anyone.'

Cyn scowled. 'You want everyone to be just like you. Happily engaged to be married, ready to settle down. Well, that's not what I want. My dreams don't involve a church, an aisle and a meringue dress.'

'I know.' Lisa gave her a sidelong look. 'Besides, you always have a computer screen safely between you and anybody male.'

Cyn got the implication and glowered. 'I am *not* scared of men.'

'Course you're not,' Lisa soothed—though her tone suggested the complete opposite.

Cyn thought, Was she scared? No. She just didn't want to make her mother's mistakes—and discover that every potential Mr Right was actually Mr Wrong. There was plenty of time to settle down. She liked her life the way it was. Work, the odd night out with colleagues, the odd night out with Lisa. Freedom to do what she wanted, when she wanted. Why change it?

'So I get a free hand?' Lisa asked.

Cyn capitulated. 'Yes. I know Max's going to the wedding as a pity date and a favour for you, but it'd be nice for it not to look like that.'

'Leave it to me,' Lisa said. 'Cynders, you shall go to the ball—and how!'

* * *

On Saturday morning, Max rang the doorbell and waited. Cyn would be wearing a navy suit, he guessed. Something businesslike. She might have let Lisa do her make-up, but he'd bet it wouldn't be much. The bare minimum—maybe a bit of lipstick.

When she opened the door, he nearly keeled over. This wasn't what he'd been expecting at all. Cyn was wearing full make-up—subtle, the barely there look, but he knew from past girlfriends just how high maintenance it was.

The first time he'd met her, she'd worn a face-pack. This was yet another mask, he'd bet. Lisa had as good as told him that Cyn was a shy, mousy geek. Homely, even. He hadn't been able to tell anything from the fluffy dressing gown and face mask—but he really hadn't thought she'd look anything like this. This woman was a starlet. Five feet two inches of pure sultriness. Real curves—and her long bias-cut skirt, matching jacket and long-sleeved, round-necked top weren't in the slightest bit demure. Okay, so he couldn't see any actual *skin* below her collar-bones, but her clothes didn't hide her shape at all. They showed it off. And what that really made him want to do was unwrap her. Layer by layer.

Not good. He was there to play a part. He definitely wasn't getting involved with his PA's best friend; any crossover between his business life and his personal life would be a disaster. He'd already done 'disaster' with Gina. And he didn't repeat his mistakes.

'Hi,' she said, looking nervous.

He unglued his tongue from the roof of his mouth. 'Hi. Ready?'

'Yes. And thanks for doing this. I owe you.'

He shrugged. 'No worries. You can fill me in properly about the wedding on the way there.'

Who was it who'd said that living well was the best revenge? Today, Michelle Wilson and her cronies would definitely get their comeuppance. Max Taylor was perfect. Slate-blue eyes that made your stomach flutter with desire. Broad shoulders, lean hips, and the kind of lower lip that made you want to take a bite. Good suit, white shirt, understated silk tie. It all said 'money' and 'taste' and 'breeding'. Things they'd said Cyn would never, ever have.

True, he wasn't actually *hers*. But they didn't need to know that.

And then she saw his car. 'This is *yours*?' Low-slung, two-seater, latest registration plate—a real boy toy.

'Yup.' He grinned. 'Like it?'

'Er—yes.' Though it was hard to climb into a car this low down when you were balancing on heels, particularly when you normally wore flats. But then she was in, the door was closed, and he was sitting beside her. His arm just brushed against her as he leaned over to do up her seat belt, and her whole body was suddenly on red alert.

Suddenly, this seemed like a bad idea. A really bad idea. If just a light, accidental touch could have this effect on her, how was she going to cope when Max started pretending to be her boyfriend?

'Let's go.' He was sensible enough to stick to the speed limits—but he also manoeuvred the car into little gaps Cyn would never have dared to go for. And he seemed to know exactly where he was going?

'Um, don't you need directions?' she asked.

He gave her a sidelong look. 'You told me where the ceremony was. I plotted the route on the Internet.'

No arguing with that. Though she noted that he hadn't printed out the route. Obviously he had an excellent memory. Well, Lisa had said his mind was really sharp.

'So, this wedding…tell me about it,' he invited.

'There isn't much to tell. I went to school with the

bride.' Cyn shrugged. 'I haven't seen Michelle Wilson in years.'

'So why did she invite you?'

'She invited practically everyone in the village.' Cyn sighed. 'I was going to say I couldn't come because I was working abroad, but my mum wanted to go.'

'Your mum?'

'My mum,' Cyn said quietly, 'used to be Mrs Wilson's cleaner.'

'Does that matter?'

'It did at my school.'

'Village schools aren't normally like that.'

She knew that. Which was why she wished she hadn't let the head persuade her into accepting the place. 'It wasn't a village school. It was a private school.' She squirmed at the memory. 'I was a scholarship kid.' His silence showed he really didn't get it. 'My uniform was second-hand, and they all knew it.' Still silence. Nope, he didn't understand—she just hadn't fitted in. Wasn't part of that set. 'I didn't do ballet or pony club, like the rest of them.'

'So *that's* why you wanted a trophy boyfriend. To fill in the chip on your shoulder.'

'I beg your pardon?' She stared at him in disbelief.

'About being from the wrong sort of background,' he said. 'Which is ridiculous. Lisa told me you have a First from Cambridge. That's enough to shut anyone up.'

He *really* didn't get it, did he? 'Not them. And it's not *me* I'm worried about. I would have just binned the invitation and sent a very short note thanking Mrs Wilson for her kind thought but saying I was unable to attend,' she said stiffly.

'So why didn't you?'

'I told you,' Cyn said. 'Because my mother wanted to go. Why she wants to see a witch like Michelle Wilson waltz down the aisle, I'll never know—but she does. And if I don't turn up, the whole bloody village will be gossiping about why. They'll turn me into some frumpy old maid who can't get a man and is too embarrassed to show my face, and they'll make snide comments that my mum's meant to overhear. I don't want them using me to be nasty to her.'

Max frowned. 'You're an IT whizkid, according to Lisa. You probably earn more than any of that lot.'

'That doesn't matter to them. They judge you on your relationships, not your career. It'll be years before I'm ready to settle down—but they'll think I'm on the shelf because I'm twenty-seven and single. For your information, I don't give a damn what they think about me. But I *do* care about them getting their knives into my mum. She's already had to put up with enough from them and their snobbery.' Cyn gritted her teeth at the memories. 'So, yes, I admit, I wanted a trophy boyfriend for today. Someone they'll all be jealous of. And then they might just start showing my mum a bit more respect. The respect she deserves.'

Max exhaled sharply. 'This is supposed to be the twenty-first century, not Victorian times!'

'This is a small village we're talking about. Where everyone knows everything about everyone, and your background matters more than who you are as a person. If you leave, the hole you leave behind stays the same shape—so when you go back, you just don't fit any more. You've changed but they won't see it.' Cyn lifted her chin. 'So if you want to back out now, I'd appreciate you pulling over so I can get the tube home and collect my own car. If I'm going to the wedding on my own, I'd rather be on time.'

'I didn't say I was backing out. Just that your background shouldn't matter.'

'Well, it does.' She blinked away the tears stinging her

eyes. This was the worst mistake she'd ever made. Turning up on her own would've been better than this. It was going to be so obvious that Max was virtually a stranger. And the witches in the village would gossip even more.

As if he'd read her mind, he said, 'If we're going to make this work, we need to get our story straight and stick to it. Best to keep as near to the truth as possible, so there's less chance of slipping up. So we met through Lisa—she's my PA and your housemate. We got talking one night, and found out we have a lot in common.'

'Like what? You're an architect and I'm an IT project manager. Our worlds don't even begin to collide.'

He shrugged. 'I imagine that building a city on a computer game's pretty similar to architecture.'

What on earth had Lisa told him about her? 'I don't write that sort of program. I do tailor-made business packages,' she said stiffly.

He said nothing, and Cyn could have kicked herself. She was being oversensitive. Seeing every comment as a slight because she knew she'd hear dig after dig after dig at the wedding. 'But, yeah, you're right. Systems architecture works on the same principle. You need a solid foundation—your base code—or the whole thing will collapse when you try to extend it.'

'What sort of businesses do you work with?' he asked.

'Anything and everything.' She smiled. 'My favourite client was a chocolatier up in Scotland.'

'Why would a chocolatier need a specialist computer system?'

'Sales and stock control. Linked to their website, so they needed a shopping-cart facility and secure payment as well. Not to mention secure data,' Cyn explained. 'I didn't do the front end—the shop you see on the website— but I did the business end of it and the interface.'

'Right. So you build computer systems like that from scratch?'

'Yes. The client tells me what they want to do, and I build them a system that will do it,' Cyn said. 'The best way is to ask questions—if the suggestion for changes comes from the client, it saves a lot of grief.'

'Oh, I'm with you there. It's the same with architecture,' Max said. 'You need to know what the room's going to be used for so you can design it properly—an office needs completely different lighting to a living room, for instance. Also, a lot depends on the natural light, the position of the windows, and the lie of the land.'

Different problems, but the same principles. She knew exactly where he was coming from. 'Ah, but I bet you don't get to sample your clients' wares,' she said with a grin.

Max grinned back. 'No, but if I did I think a chocolatier would be my favourite, too. Especially if I got to try new flavours.'

'I did, and they were fabulous,' Cyn said. 'Though Lisa's desperate for me to work with a shoe shop.'

'She *would* be. Lisa and her shoes.' He rolled his eyes. 'I swear she keeps our local designer shop in business single-handedly.' He smiled. 'Lisa tells me you're always being head-hunted.'

'Um, yes. But I like what I'm doing now. If I worked for just one company, I'd have to stay put all the time and I'd only be able to work with one system. RCS is a consultancy, so I get to work with different systems, I design things from scratch, and I get to do the troubleshooting as well.'

'And that's what you like? The variety?'

'Absolutely.' She nodded. 'I love troubleshooting. Computer forensics—tracing your way through a problem back to the source, then fixing it. But I like doing the other stuff as well. I want to stretch myself, so I've applied for a promotion. What about you?'

'I used to work in a consultancy. But I went solo nearly three years back. This way I get to choose the jobs I really, really want to do. I specialise in listed buildings.'

'So you don't design things from scratch?'

'Not really. I work on restoration of buildings that have been neglected and need careful handling, or on designing extensions that are in keeping with listed buildings. Which means using original materials as much as possible.' He smiled. 'I can be very, very boring about my job. Let's just say I know every reclamation place and specialist contractor within a fifty-mile radius of London.'

She smiled back. The air was definitely clearer between them. 'So you're a traditionalist when it comes to architecture, then?'

'I can appreciate modern buildings,' he said. 'But old buildings are my real love. I would have *paid* to work on a property like Ightham Mote in Kent, where you got to see the craftsmanship of several centuries. I was lucky enough to see the restoration in progress. D'you know they didn't just work to the last set of changes that had been made to the building? They went right back to the original—and then made the changes exactly as they were done over the years. Even using the same methods and same materials. That's restoration at its best—how it *should* be done.'

Wow. This was a man who felt the same way about his job as she did about hers. 'Sounds fascinating.'

'Most people don't see the point—I mean, why build the original if you're only going to change it the following week? But restoring it that way gives the building integrity.'

'And that's how *you* do it?'

He nodded. 'Where I can. The good thing is, my clients feel the same way.'

'And if they don't, you don't tender?'

'I can't work with people who buy a building just to show they can afford a listed place, or who buy it as an investment. They have to love their building. Really care about it.' He shook himself. 'And I'm on my pet hobby-horse. I'd better shut up. What else do we have in common?'

'Music?' she suggested.

'Sounds good to me. I work to classical music. Piano, mainly—Einaudi and Mozart.'

The complete opposite to her. 'Ah. I work to pop.'

'Slushy ballads. The stuff you were playing the other night.'

His tone of voice told her he couldn't stand it. 'So what do you listen to, for pleasure?' she asked.

'Rock.'

She groaned. 'As in dinosaur rock?'

'Classic,' he corrected with a grin.

'At least you can sing along to it, I suppose. Which is marginally better than techno. I can't stand that drum and bass stuff.'

'Me neither,' he admitted.

'So there must be some middle ground. How about something ambient? Nick Drake?' she suggested.

'Works for me,' he said.

Her surprise must have been really obvious, because he added, 'He was a superb guitarist. Not that I play.'

'Me neither.' And she'd been the only one in her class not to play the piano or violin. Her mum hadn't been able to afford the lessons, let alone the instrument. She shook herself. *Not now.* 'So what do we do when we go out?' she asked. 'Watch films?'

'Fine. Action movies?'

Just what she'd expected him to like. Though she

agreed with him, there. She liked slushy ballads, but she hated the girly films Lisa dragged her to see on the pretext that one of her friends was an extra in it. *'Star Wars,'* she suggested. 'And I made Lisa come with me to one of those *Lord of the Rings* showings—you know, the one where they do all three films in a row, the director's cut, rather than the cinema cut. Lisa only went on condition I fed her a ton of ice cream and called her "Mrs Aragorn" for the next month.'

Max laughed. 'Oh, that's classic. I'll remember that one next time she nags me. Anything else? What do *you* do in the evenings?'

'Work,' she admitted. 'You?'

'Depends. Might work late, might go to the gym, might go out for a beer with some friends.'

'Pubs and clubs?' She grimaced. 'Oh, yawn.'

'Clubbing's boring. And in those types of places I spend too much time spotting the flaws in the architecture.'

Not chatting up women? Hmm. Lisa had said Max never dated the same woman more than two or three times. He was a player. Not that it should bother Cyn. She wasn't looking at him as real boyfriend material.

'I think it's best if we say we've only been together a couple of weeks. We know the important things about each other, but we're taking time now to get to know each other a little more,' he suggested.

'Right. Hopefully they'll buy that.'

'Course they will. Just smile at me as if you're Lisa and I'm Aragorn.'

She wasn't sure if he was teasing or not; his voice was completely deadpan. Then he grinned, and Cyn relaxed. This was going to work. Max had confidence enough for both of them. And if anyone questioned them, all he had to do was grin like that. It'd scramble every female brain cell in the place, and they'd forget what they'd asked.

Cynthia Reynolds was going to return home as Cinderella—and wipe the ugly smiles off quite a few faces…

CHAPTER THREE

By THE time Max turned into the tree-lined drive to the country house hotel where the wedding was being held, he and Cyn had worked out enough details of their 'relationship' to sound convincing. But there was still something niggling him.

'Cyn?' he asked, when he'd parked.

'Mmm-hmm?'

'We're meant to be a couple. We're at the beginning of a relationship. People are going to expect me to put my arm round you. If you flinch, it'll be obvious that this is a set-up.'

She shook her head. 'I won't flinch.'

'How do you know?'

'I just do.'

Nope. He wasn't buying that. Especially as she wasn't actually looking at him. She clearly didn't trust her reactions, either. And he knew from business that if you didn't prepare properly, you wouldn't have a chance in hell of getting the contract. This was the same sort of thing. 'I'd be happier if we did some preparation.'

She met his gaze, this time, and nodded. 'What did you have in mind?'

'Nothing too scary.' He released both their seat belts. 'Lean forward.'

She did, and he slid his arm round her, resting his left hand on her left shoulder.

She flinched.

'See? Do that in public, and we're in trouble.'

She sighed. 'So what do you suggest?'

'This.' He shouldn't do it, he *knew* he shouldn't do it. But he couldn't resist. He let his left hand slide from her shoulder to the nape of her neck. Tension radiated from her; slowly, gently, he stroked the nape of her neck.

She shivered, and tipped her head back ever so slightly.

It was all the invitation he needed. He bent his head and touched his mouth to hers. Lightly, like the kiss of a butterfly's wings, just sliding his mouth along the curve of her lower lip. When she didn't pull back, he kissed her again. One light kiss at each corner of that delectable mouth, and one right in the centre.

No flinching, this time, but he definitely felt a tiny shiver run up her spine against his fingers.

This time, when he bent his head, his mouth coaxed hers. Tiny nibbles against her lower lip, encouraging her to open her mouth. She remained absolutely still, as if she didn't trust herself to move; then, finally, she opened her mouth under his and let him deepen the kiss.

Oh. My. God. Cyn had been kissed before, but Max was in another league. His right hand was flat against her stomach. Just resting there. No pressure, no demands; just waiting for her to make the next move. Her breasts felt heavy and her nipples were so tight, they almost hurt. She wanted his hand to slide over her silky top, cup her breast. More, she wanted his hand to slide *under* her top, so they were skin to skin. She wanted his thumb to rub against her nipple. Better still, she wanted him to use his mouth. She wanted to grab his hand and place it exactly where she needed to be touched.

But they were supposed to be going to a wedding. Right here, right now. And she needed to look respectable. Cyn Reynolds, business hotshot. Except Max had just kissed all her lipstick off and she was going to look…embarrassing. She did *not* want to get out of this car and walk into the wedding looking as if she'd been necking in the car park! Even though, technically, she had been.

She slid her hands to his shoulders and pushed.

Instantly, he stopped kissing her. Backed off.

'Cyn?' His voice was husky, his pupils were huge and there was a slash of colour across his cheekbones. Clearly he was just as turned on as she was.

'We're supposed to be going to a wedding,' she croaked.

'Yeah.'

But his gaze was still fixed on her mouth. A hungry gaze. This was a man who wanted more—much more. Panic flared through her. Not here…not now! 'We're going to be late,' she said shakily. And she'd better sort out her lipstick. Repair the damage, make herself look respectable again. She pulled the visor down, and stared in surprise at her reflection in the vanity mirror.

The lipstick was still in place.

'Something wrong?' Max asked.

'I, um, no.' How was that possible? How, when he'd kissed her so thoroughly? She sneaked a quick glance. And no, there wasn't a scrap of lipstick on his face, either. Huh? Was this all some kind of weird dream, and her alarm was going to wake her any second?

'Cyn.'

Unwillingly, she met his gaze. 'What?'

'You don't normally wear make-up, do you?'

Hopefully, said make-up was enough to hide the colour she could feel scorching her face. 'Course I do.'

'Not for a long time, then. You can buy lipstick nowadays

that's designed to stay put. And my guess is that Lisa chose that sort for you, so you wouldn't have to worry about renewing your lipstick every time you took a sip of your drink.'

'Uh-huh.'

'You look…'

Max's mouth dried. Her eyes were huge and dark; her lips were just that tiniest bit pouty. As if she'd just been kissed. As if she wanted to be kissed again. And his whole body was saying yes, yes, yes, *do it*!

No.

Cyn wasn't even his type—he always went out with tall skinny blondes or redheads. Probably because Gina had been little and dark and soft. Like Cyn. Too much like Cyn. He wasn't going to get in that kind of situation again. 'Stop worrying. You look fine,' he said gruffly. 'Let's go.'

Fine?

Sheesh. It was like when you were covered in teenage spots and someone told you that you had beautiful eyes or a lovely smile. They didn't mention the fact that your face looked like the moon through a half-focused telescope. Saying you looked 'fine' was just as bad as saying you looked 'nice' or 'all right'; the kind of lukewarm compliment that was given when someone felt too guilty to say that you looked terrible.

She'd wanted to look stunning.

Lisa had done her best, but she hadn't had A-class material to work with in the first place. Too short, too plump, too…ordinary. Cyn stiffened her backbone. Well, she might *look* ordinary, but that didn't mean she *was* ordinary. She was every bit as good as her old school acquaintances. And if she was going to convince them that Max Taylor was really hers, she'd better act as if she believed it.

So she pinned a smile to her face. And when Max opened the car door for her, she let him help her put on the cute jacket that matched her skirt, then slid her arm through the crook of his. Cyn-derella Reynolds was going to the ball.

'Cynthia! Hello, sweetie.' The redhead bore down on them and gave Cyn an air kiss. Just the kind of thing Max hated. From the brief flash of distaste on Cyn's face, it seemed as if she wasn't too keen on it, either.

'Aren't you going to introduce us to your fr...?' The other woman's over-sugared tones died as she glanced at Max. Almost, he thought, as if she didn't quite believe Cynthia had turned up to the wedding with anyone at all, let alone someone like him.

'My friend? Of course,' Cyn said politely. 'Max, this is Ella Jameson. Ella, Max Taylor.'

Max just about managed to keep the smile on his face as the redhead looked him up and down again. Checking out the fabric of his suit, the polish of his shoes, even the cut of his hair. He'd seen this before, in clients. Beneath that oh-so-sweet smile, Ella Jameson was a predator. If the rest of this pack was like that, no wonder Cyn had wanted a trophy boyfriend for the day.

'Actually, it's Ella Hopcroft-Brown,' Ella corrected. Max noted that she made sure they both saw the enormous solitaire and the wedding band on her left hand. 'So, what do you do, Max?'

At Ella's snooty tones, Max was tempted—really tempted—to claim he was a bricklayer. Had he not felt Cyn's tiny betraying shiver, he would have said it, too. Instead, he smiled sweetly. 'I'm an architect. I specialise in the renovation of listed buildings.'

'Oh, how *interesting*.'

Yeah, and he'd bet the 'interest' she had in mind wasn't cerebral. It was measured in percentage points and bank balances. Listed buildings meant serious money. That was what would make him interesting to a woman like Ella Hopcroft-Brown.

'And you're a computer operator, aren't you, Cyn?'

'Something like that.'

Max was about to leap to Cyn's defence when he heard the resignation in her tone. And Ella was already moving away, saying, 'Catch you later, sweetie. Ciao.'

'What a bitch,' Max muttered. 'Why didn't you tell her what you really do?'

'No point.' Cyn sounded weary. 'They all know where I did my degree. And it still doesn't make a difference, because they know where I come from. And that's where I'll always be, in their eyes. I told you before, in a village, you have your set place. And even if you change, your place doesn't.'

Which meant you didn't fit any more. On the way here, he'd accused her of having a chip on her shoulder, about being the poor-girl-made-good. Now he realised she hadn't been chippy at all. She'd been spot on. He could see the heads turning, the double takes, the little nudges and whispers. From Ella's reaction, he could guess what they were saying: 'Isn't that Cynthia Reynolds?' Then dismissive comments would follow, about how she'd been at school: the outsider.

Which she still was.

Cyn knew it, too. He could see it in her face. 'You okay?' he asked.

She gave him a smile, but he had a feeling she was close to bolting from the room. Well, he wasn't going to let her. She was going to stay, and prove to this nest of vipers that she was every bit as good as they were.

At least the older generation seemed to look more kindly on her. There were smiles and nods of recognition. And then a woman stood up and walked towards her.

Cyn's mum. Had to be. An older, plainer version of Cyn, but then she smiled. A smile full of love and pride and happiness. The kind of smile mothers reserved for their children. And her whole face changed: she was beautiful.

'Cyn! You look fabulous. Turn round.'

Cyn dutifully pirouetted.

The older woman's smile broadened. 'The colours suit you. I would've bet serious money on you wearing a grey or navy suit today.'

'Mum, please.' Cyn sounded pained.

Her mother hugged her. 'You've always been beautiful. I'm glad you're letting other people see it, too.'

'*Mum.*' Cyn wriggled; her expression was a mixture of embarrassment and pleasure.

'Mothers are meant to embarrass their children. But you *do* look lovely, Cyn. Very glamorous and London.' Cyn's mother squeezed her hand. 'My gorgeous girl.'

Cyn clearly wanted to distract her mother, because then she began her introductions. 'Mum, this is Max Taylor. A friend. Max, this is my mother, Stacey Reynolds.'

'Pleased to meet you.' Stacey shook his hand and smiled, but he was aware that she was assessing him. Checking that he wasn't going to hurt her little girl. She didn't say it in words, but her eyes said it for her. *Treat my daughter right, or I'll break every single bone in your body. Twice.*

'Pleased to meet you, too,' he said.

So where was Cyn's dad? Or maybe she didn't have one. Maybe Stacey was a widow. Or a divorcee—there were no rings on her left hand. Well, he wasn't going to push Cyn for an explanation. It was none of his business. But if his guess was right, that was another reason why Cyn hadn't fitted in. Why she'd made herself look almost invisible. It was so she wouldn't attract attention, or the negative comments that went with it.

Max decided to be polite, took part in the social chit-chat—and made sure that his arm stayed firmly round Cyn's shoulders. If anyone was going to make a sly comment, they'd have to get past him first.

'I love weddings,' Stacey said as they walked into the room for the ceremony.

Cyn and Max exchanged a glance; *they* didn't.

When the bride flounced down the aisle, Max tightened his fingers against Cyn's shoulders. He knew the type: blonde, gorgeous, and needing to be the centre of attention, the one everyone thought as 'the best' in everything. His guess was that Michelle Wilson had been number one in class in everything until Cyn had come along and knocked her off the top spot academically, and Michelle had taken her revenge by prodding Cyn where she'd been most vulnerable, making her a social outcast.

Funny. He barely knew Cyn. And here he was, wanting to take up cudgels on her behalf. Not that he was getting involved. It was just the ridiculously formal wedding atmosphere—people wearing tailcoats, top hats and corsages, and behaving as stiffly as their clothes. He'd have felt that same protectiveness about anyone in this situation—wouldn't he?

As the day went on, Cyn looked more and more trapped. But Max wasn't going to let her run from here with her tail between her legs. When she left, it would be when *she* chose to leave, not because she'd been driven out. And she'd walk tall when she left.

So he stuck to her side like glue. Schmoozed as if the

contract of his dreams—the restoration of a huge tumble-down manor house to its original state, with an unlimited budget—was at stake. By the time the wedding breakfast was over, the speeches had been made, the bride and groom had done the first dance and everyone was chatting at the edge of the dance floor in little groups, Max had charmed every single female in the room—including the bride and her mother. He noted with satisfaction that they were all giving Cyn envious glances.

Just you wait, he thought. It's only going to get better.

If she didn't get two minutes to herself, Cyn knew she would scream. She hated being on show like this. She hated smiling and smiling, and pretending everything was fine, when she knew they all still despised her as much as they always had.

She excused herself to go to the loo, and was sitting quietly in a cubicle, just glad of the breathing space, when she heard a door open and footsteps echoing.

'I can't believe that was Cynthia Reynolds,' a voice said.

Ella Hopcroft-Brown. Cyn recognised the voice.

'How on earth did she afford those clothes? She was always dirt poor.'

Cyn stayed absolutely still. Here it came. The knife was about to go in.

'And the guy she's with—he's really hot. I never thought *she'd* end up with someone like that,' the second woman said.

A touch of envy. Better. She relaxed.

'*If* she's really with him,' Ella said.

Cyn stiffened again.

'How do you mean?' the other woman asked.

'Look at their body language, sweetie.' 'Chelle pointed

it out. He puts his arm round her, but she doesn't lean into him. So it's an act. Bet you anything he's married to a friend who's lent him to her for the day.'

Now was her cue, to walk out of the cubicle, act cool, and tell them that Max gave her better orgasms than either of them would ever experience in ten lifetimes.

Except she was too angry to trust herself to speak. And, by the time she'd done enough deep breathing to cool down again, they'd switched to another topic. If she came out and said anything now, she'd look stupid for having sat there and eavesdropped.

Too late.

So she'd wait it out.

She waited.

And waited.

How could women spend such a long time painting their lips or brushing their hair? *How?*

But at last she heard footsteps and the door closing, and the room was silent again.

Cyn counted silently to ten, then unlocked the door, washed her hands, scowled at her reflection, and returned to Max.

She leaned over his shoulder, trying to make it look as if she were whispering sweet nothings into his ear. 'We need to leave quietly.'

'Why? Did you punch the bride on the nose, or something?'

'No. All her cronies know we're fake.'

'What?'

'Ella and another woman. I heard them talking about it in the loo.'

'Right.' He took her hands from his shoulders, kissed her fingers, and stood up, still holding her hands. 'Let's show them.'

'What?'

'Prove we're a couple.'

Cyn remembered the kiss in the car and a shiver ran up her spine. 'We can't.'

'Why not?' he asked, as he manoeuvred her away from the chair.

'Because I've just borrowed you for the day.' And they'd guessed it straight away.

'So?' He gave her a lopsided grin filled with mischief. 'Can you dance?'

She shook her head. 'I've got two left feet. Why?'

'No problem. Just follow my lead.'

'Max—'

He held one hand up, forestalling her words. 'Just stay here for a second. And do *not* run away, under any circumstances. We're going to do some serious eye-poking.'

She stayed put, too confused to move—and then she saw him moving towards the DJ. Oh, no. Please don't let him announce anything over the microphone. Please.

She wanted to run up to the stage, kick Max in the shins and tell the DJ to ignore everything he'd said, but her legs refused to comply.

'What have you done?' she whispered when he returned.

'Don't worry. This is going to be fun.'

'Fun?'

'Yeah. Trust me.' He grinned. 'Ever seen *Dirty Dancing*?'

She stared at him, horror mounting. 'I told you, I can't dance.'

'And I told you, don't worry. I can,' he said softly. 'I took salsa lessons to impress a girl I lost my heart to, when I was seventeen.'

'Oh, my God. You're going to make me salsa, when I can't dance. You're going to make me a laughing stock for the rest of my days.' Not just her, either. Her mother was never going to be able to walk into a shop in the town again, without someone commenting about her daughter's embarrassing performance at the Wilson wedding.

'*Au contraire*. I'm going to wipe the smiles off some faces. Walk with me, babe,' he said, in a hammy accent that would ordinarily have made her laugh. Right now, panic was gluing up every single muscle. She couldn't move.

He sighed, leaned forward and touched his lips to hers. Lightly. A promise. 'Trust me. We can do this.'

The first notes of 'I've Had The Time of My Life' filtered through the room.

Oh, no. He was going to make her dance to *that* tune. The one all the girls had sighed over in their teens, wishing that Patrick Swayze were theirs. She couldn't do it.

Earth, please open and swallow me right now, she thought.

Still, at least the dance floor was reasonably crowded. There was a chance they'd escape notice. Then they could leave. Fast. Preferably after the first step.

'You hate this sort of music,' she hissed frantically.

'Doesn't matter. Just follow my lead,' he whispered, and began to dance with her.

It was amazing. Like nothing else she'd ever done. A touch of his hand on her hips here, a flick of his wrist there, and she was spinning round the room with him. Lighter than air, arching back over his arm, then spinning into his arms so that they closed round her. They were dancing cheek to cheek—except he was standing behind her, his arms wrapped round her waist and his hips moulded against her, and… Oh, this was barely decent. Mrs Wilson would have a fit at two of her guests virtually having sex on the dance floor!

But the room shrank until there was nothing except her, Max and the music. Max, who spun her back round to face him and kept his eyes on her as if there were nobody else in the whole room. Max, whose hands were directing her to move in a way she'd never, ever been able to do before. Max, whose eyes glittered with desire.

And, right now, he was all hers.

The music finished; he pulled her into his arms, bent her backwards, and kissed her. Thoroughly.

Time stopped.

The universe collapsed.

When his mouth left hers, she became aware of a noise. Applause. Everyone was *clapping*. They were in the middle of the dance floor, a spotlight was somehow trained on them, and everyone was clapping.

How long had they been dancing solo?

How long had Max been kissing her?

Why wasn't the earth opening up and swallowing her?

Cyn felt like a rabbit trapped in headlights. Just let the lights go down. Please. Let them go down and let her slink out of the room, and she'd never darken the doorstep again.

Max didn't seem bothered. He just put his arm round her shoulders and shepherded her off the floor.

'Mission accomplished,' he whispered in her ear. 'All the women want to kill you, all the men want to be me, and there won't be any more rumours about you and me not being a couple.'

Uh. She couldn't even string two thoughts together right now, let alone two spoken words.

His lips brushed her earlobe. 'You owe me a favour, Cyn Reynolds. And I'll collect…some time.'

CHAPTER FOUR

SHE wasn't sure whether it was a threat or a promise. Or whether it scared her more or thrilled her. Collect...in what way?

Did he mean he expected her to go to bed with him to say thank you?

No. Max Taylor wouldn't need to call in any favours for a woman to go to bed with him. All he'd have to do was look at her. Those blue, blue eyes would do it all for him. One little, questioning look.

If he asked her...

Though he wouldn't. He was Cyn's trophy boyfriend for the day. That was the deal. They'd said nothing about sex. So why couldn't she stop looking at his mouth? Why was it, even when they were dancing fast, she found herself accidentally brushing against him? Why was her spine tingling like this?

Max lifted a glass of champagne from the tray of a passing waiter, and handed it to her. 'Dutch courage,' he whispered.

To help her deal with the wedding reception? Or to help her deal with him?

She shut the thought off as soon as it formed. 'Why aren't you having one?'

'I'm driving,' he reminded her.

So he was. And Cyn didn't need the champagne. She needed a cold shower. Especially when she noticed that Max was watching her mouth, too. But a cold shower wasn't an option, so she gulped her drink instead. The bubbles from the champagne burst against her lips, reminding her of the way Max had kissed her. Oh, this was bad. She wanted Max to kiss her again.

But did *he* want the same?

She'd gone nervous on him, Max thought, and the champagne hadn't helped. Maybe he shouldn't have danced with her like that. But it had been the best thing he could think of at the time; dancing with her, kissing her in front of everyone to prove that they were an item.

Problem was, now he wanted more. A lot more. He wanted to dance with her in this room. And dance with her when they were all alone. In a room that contained a big, wide, soft bed.

Dance with her horizontally…

But Cynthia Reynolds wasn't a player. For her, a date wouldn't be just a good night out, a chance to have fun. It would be part of something more serious. He wasn't ready for serious. Might *never* be ready for serious. He should keep his distance.

All the same, Max didn't stop dancing with her—except for the few moments when Cyn said goodbye to her mother. And he didn't let anyone else dance with her, either.

'Sorry. I'm greedy about my woman,' he said, when one annoyingly persistent man asked for the third time.

Cyn knew Max was just protecting her, in case the other man couldn't dance as well as he could. But the words still thrilled her.

Greedy about my woman.

As if he wanted her. Really wanted her. Wanted to touch and stroke and kiss and taste. As if it would take a long, long time to slake his hunger. As if he'd devour her bit by bit.

It didn't matter what was playing. Fast, slow…whatever, Max kept her close. Little touches on her hips, her back, her shoulders. Spinning her round so she ended up with her back against his chest and his arms wrapped round her waist. Dipping his head to steal a kiss. Rubbing his nose against hers.

By the last dance, she could almost believe that he found her as attractive as she found him. Everything exploded into her senses. The way his body felt against hers. His scent. The deep rumble of his laugh. That mischievous twinkle in his eyes. The promise of his mouth. The touch of his hands.

She forgot about being sensible, about being safe, about not looking for Mr Right or Mr Right Now. All she could think about was Max. *Just kiss me*, she thought as the DJ played the last song, a slow, soft number. She ached for this man to kiss her properly. For the heat to flare up between them and scorch the rest of the world away.

She stroked the back of his neck, hoping the movement of her fingers would make him take the hint. That he'd dip his head, touch his mouth to hers. Lightly, softly, just brushing his mouth over hers. Teasing her until her mouth opened beneath his. And then he'd—

The lights came up, and she could have howled in disappointment. Just a few seconds more. That was all she'd needed. Just a few seconds more and Max would have kissed her. But, no. The lights were on full and the DJ was telling everyone to drive safely and making the kind of slushy comments DJs always made at weddings.

Now it was midnight. Time to leave. When Max slid her jacket round her shoulders and didn't move his arm away again, Cyn slid her arm round his waist. All right, so he wasn't *actually* hers; but he was hers until he dropped her back in London. She was going to enjoy the last hour or so before the carriage-turning-back-into-pumpkin thing happened.

Just as they were walking down the steps from the hotel, they heard a bang and a sharp splintering sound.

'Sounds as if someone's just lost some lights—and put a dent into someone else's car,' Max said. 'Ouch.'

His smile of sympathy faded, though, when they got closer to the car park.

Because the dented car happened to be a low-slung, silver-grey two-seater.

And the 'dent' was a little bit more serious than that. The bonnet had crumpled, the headlights were out—no way could he drive the car home safely in the middle of the night.

He swore under his breath. Cyn tightened her arm round his waist in sympathy. Max's car had been pristine, and now it was crumpled. Very crumpled.

'You'd better go inside,' he said. 'It's cold out here and this might take some time to sort out.'

Cyn bridled; she was far from being a helpless female and didn't like being treated as one. It must have shown on her face, because he added, 'We might be in for a bit of a wait and there's no point in both of us standing around out here, getting cold. If you could sweet-talk someone into making us some coffee, I'd really appreciate it.'

Okay. She could do that.

A waitress had just delivered a pot of coffee and two cups when Max walked into the hotel's reception area.

'Sorted?' she asked, noting the grim set of his face.

'Want the bad news, or the bad news?'

She spread her hands. 'Looks like it's going to be the bad news. Hit me with it, pardner.'

'It's Saturday night. The rescue-and-repair people have loads of call-outs and won't get to us for at least four hours.'

She was quick to do the maths. 'Quarter past four in the morning.'

'*If* they don't get held up.' He sat on the plush sofa next to her. 'And the journey has to be one unbroken trip. They'll drop the car to the coach works, or to your place or to mine, but they won't go to all three—especially because Bayswater and Islington aren't exactly next to each other.'

'Which means calling a taxi when we get back to the coach works, so it'll be a good six hours until we get home.' She poured him a coffee and pushed the jug of milk towards him.

He added milk and took a swig of coffee. 'I've got a better idea. We could stay overnight—then we'll get the rescue van to pick us up at a reasonable time in the morning.'

'If the hotel's got any rooms left.' The Wilsons had probably block-booked it.

'I'll check,' Max said.

He returned a few moments later with the news. 'They have one room left. A double.'

Cyn felt the smile wipe off her face. One room. A *double*. Which meant that she was going to have to share a bed with Max.

'Problems, Cynthia?'

Oh, great. The one person she really had to be polite to—the woman who'd employed her mother for years and years. Who'd insisted on giving her handouts—and made sure that everyone knew Mrs Wilson had been gracious enough to give Stacey Reynolds her cast-offs.

Cyn forced herself to smile at the mother of the bride. 'Nothing we can't deal with, Mrs Wilson. Unfortunately someone backed into Max's car, which is now undriveable, so we'll have to stay here until the rescue van turns up in the morning. Max was just booking us a room—weren't you, darling?'

'Yes.' He leaned over to kiss the top of her head. 'I'll be back in a minute, sweetheart.'

She was secretly delighted to see how taken aback Mrs Wilson was. No doubt she thought Stacey's daughter couldn't afford to stay at somewhere as expensive as this, and it was a surprise to see Cyn looking so blasé about it. Not to mention the fact that Swotty Cynthia happened to have a gorgeous boyfriend.

'Lovely wedding, Mrs Wilson. It must have taken quite some organising,' Max added over his shoulder.

Make that charming as well as gorgeous, Cyn thought. Plus he'd just given her a subtle reminder that her manners needed to be impeccable in front of this woman. 'Yes, it was amazing,' she said as Max headed for the reception desk. 'Thank you for inviting us,' she said sweetly. 'It was so kind of you to let me bring a guest.'

'Michelle would have addressed the invitation to both of you, but your mother wasn't sure of your boyfriend's name.'

Cyn heard the subtext there. Meaning that her mum had tried to protect her from sniping, but the village gossips had taken her reticence to mean that Cyn was single. A failure, in their eyes. Cyn gave what she hoped was a nonchalant shrug. 'That's living in the city for you. You know a lot of people.' Which hopefully would give the impression that she had a dizzy social life and stop any deeper probing.

'Max is a lovely boy,' Mrs Wilson said. 'So charming.'

Before she could stop herself, Cyn found herself purring, 'Yes, he's quite a man.'

Oh, Lord. Mrs Wilson looked scandalised. And then there was the faintest hint of 'like mother, like daughter' in her eyes. Given what had happened earlier on the dance floor, Cyn might just as well have carved the word 'trollop' onto her forehead.

'So have you known him long, Cynthia?'

Uh-oh. Here it came. The inquisition. Well, they'd prepared for this. She knew the script. 'Not that long. He's my best friend's boss.'

'Oh.' Meaning: *So you're a gold-digger.*

'We met a couple of weeks ago. Our paths don't normally cross because I'm fairly busy at work. I'm away quite a bit, seeing clients.'

'I thought you were a computer operator?' Mrs Wilson said.

Cyn smiled. 'Sort of. I do sit in front of a keyboard, a lot of the time—but what I actually do is design computer systems. I write the programs that make them work. So if you've bought chocolates or something on the Internet, you've used the kind of system I build. It sends your order to the shop and it keeps your money safe.'

'Oh. I thought you… Well.' Mrs Wilson gave a dismissive shrug. 'And Max is an architect, isn't he?'

Cyn nodded. 'He specialises in listed buildings. And he's among the best in his field. He's won awards for his work—because he cares about what he does.'

'So how did you meet?'

Just as well they'd prepared this. 'As I said, he's my best friend's boss. He dropped her home after a late meeting, and I happened to be in, for once. We got chatting, and…well.' She spread her hands. 'We just hit it off.'

'We certainly did.' Max came to stand beside her. 'In

my job, you learn to look below the surface and see what's really there. And once I'd got past the image of this quiet woman in a business suit—'

What? He'd never seen her in her work clothes!

'—I discovered a girl with the sweetest nature. As well as a brain that puts mine to shame.'

Cyn flushed. 'Max. You have more letters after your name than I do.'

'But not a First from Cambridge. You must be so proud of your daughter's schoolfriend, Mrs Wilson,' Max said relentlessly. 'Because she's made quite a name for herself in London. Her work's really respected and she gets head-hunted practically every week.'

'Oh, um, of course. Cynthia was always bright,' Mrs Wilson said, looking slightly flustered.

Cyn was cringing inwardly. He'd gone too far. 'Max,' she muttered through clenched teeth.

He gave her a don't-worry-it's-fine smile.

'Well, I'll leave you to sort out your room,' Mrs Wilson said. 'Goodnight.'

'Goodnight. And thanks once again for inviting us,' Cyn said hastily.

They watched her walk away. 'I can't believe you said that to her,' Cyn said in an outraged whisper.

'Relax. It did the trick. And let's just say that the round hole they've kept for you might have started to get four corners.' He gave her a half-smile. 'I think the party's over. Shall we go up?'

For a heart-stopping moment, she'd thought he was going to say, 'Shall we go to bed?'

'Sure,' she said, hoping that she sounded completely cool and calm. Inside, every single one of her neurons was on red alert and shrieking an alarm call. She was actually going to spend the night in the same room as Max. The same *bed* as Max. She remembered his words at the end of their first dance and it made her head spin. *You owe me a favour, Cyn Reynolds. And I'll collect…some time.*

Would he expect to collect that favour tonight? And how?

Oh, Lord. Her mouth felt as if it had been pegged open in the middle of a windy day in the Sahara Desert. She already knew that Max Taylor had dated women who were far, far more glamorous than she was. Which meant he'd been to bed with women who knew what they were doing. Women who didn't wear tights that held in their wobbly bits. Women who didn't have wobbly bits in the first place!

Not good. She was way out of her league, here. Maybe she should pre-empt the situation and offer to spend the night in the hotel lounge while he took the room. Except it was already too late for that because he was ushering her up to their room.

When Max opened the door and stood aside for her, the panic went up another notch. The room was small—so small that it didn't even have a comfy chair, let alone the sofa she'd hoped to sleep on. And it was dominated by the double bed set right in the middle.

The double bed she was going to have to share with him.

The door clicked behind them, and suddenly there wasn't enough air in the room.

When Max closed the gap between them and slid his arms round her waist, pulling her back against his body, there wasn't enough air in her lungs, either.

'Cyn.' He brushed his lips against the sensitive spot just behind her ear. 'Stop panicking.'

'I'm not panicking.'

'You are, too. If I put my hand over your heart, I bet it'd be beating twice as fast as normal.'

His hand over her heart. Which would mean he would be touching her breast. Through her clothes? Skin to skin?

A tremor ran through her at the thought.

'We're sharing a bed.' Another brush of his lips.

Could knees actually *melt*? Or were they just rewriting the laws of physics, between them?

'We're adults.'

Oh, yes. And she couldn't remember the last time she'd felt this female.

'We've no commitments elsewhere.'

Young, free, single. He was spelling it out for her. *They were going to have sex.*

'There's no reason why we can't…'

Make love.

'…be responsible.'

What? Had she just heard that right? Or had she heard what she wanted to hear? What she *didn't* want to hear, at the same time.

This time, he kissed the nape of her neck. Funny. She'd had no idea it was an erogenous zone, until now. And when you touched an erogenous zone, that made people do things. That was the only reason she was pressing back against him, right now. The only reason why she'd forgotten how to speak. The only reason why she couldn't open her eyes.

'There's no reason why we can't…'

Oh, yes. Another one of those lovely, soft, promising caresses. If he kept this up, she'd agree to absolutely anything.

'… make love.'

He'd said it.

'But there's something you should know.'

What? He'd already said he had no commitments. Had he changed his mind?

'I don't expect you to have sex with me, just because we're sharing a bed. It's been a long day. We're both tired. You're stressed.'

So was he—his precious car had just been crunched. And didn't all the women's magazines say that sex was the best way to relieve stress?

'Stop worrying. I'm not going to pressure you into anything you don't want to do.'

That was the point. She *did* want to. But she didn't want to make a fool of herself.

'Go take a long, hot shower,' he advised. 'It'll relax you.'

Was he going to join her? She quivered at the thought.

Another kiss, and then she was aware that his arms were no longer round her. There was actual space between them. This was where she was meant to make a smart, funny comment, right? Except…she didn't trust her mouth not to come out with something different. Something desperate.

Today she was supposed to be an urban sophisticate. And an urban sophisticate wouldn't beg a man to kiss her. Even if he did have the sexiest mouth in the world.

'Just don't use all the hot water,' he added.

Oh. So he *wasn't* planning to join her, then.

Just as well she hadn't flung herself at him and embarrassed them both. 'I'll try not to.' With a silent command to her knees to unmelt—and unmelt right that second—she walked as coolly as she could to the bathroom. As if sharing a hotel room with a virtual stranger didn't bother her in the slightest.

And locked the bathroom door behind her.

Luckily, this was the kind of hotel that supplied its guests with plenty of toiletries. She showered, then rinsed out her underwear and left it to dry on the radiator.

Then it hit her. *What was she going to wear?* Surely

there was a bathrobe. This had to be the kind of place that left you big, fluffy bathrobes behind the bathroom door.

Wrong.

She stared at her damp towel. Why couldn't it have been a bath sheet, something that she could have wrapped very securely round her, sarong-style, and it would have covered her from her armpits to the bottom of her calves? But no. It was an ordinary-sized bath towel. One that, given her curves, would only just wrap round her. And which came well above her knees.

It was that or nothing.

Short of telling Max to close his eyes and turn off the lights… No. She wasn't going to make an issue of it. She was going to be cool about it. Really cool.

And she nearly made it. Until she walked out of the bathroom and saw Max sitting on the bed. He'd shed his suit jacket and tie, and his white shirt was completely undone, revealing a washboard stomach and a muscular chest with a light sprinkling of hair. Not too much to be off-putting; just enough to make her want to run her fingers across his pecs. But it was the shirt that did it. Who was it who said something about 'a sweet disorder in the dress'? Half dressed was definitely sexy. Sexy, because it hinted at all sorts of possibilities.

She hoped she wasn't drooling. She really, really hoped she wasn't drooling. Making an effort to look casual, she sauntered into the room. 'Bathroom's all yours,' she said.

'Thanks.'

There was a pause. A long, *long* pause. Then she made the mistake of actually looking at him. His pupils were huge. Wasn't that meant to be a sign of desire? And the way he ran just the tip of his tongue along his lower lip: as if he were tasting something. Tasting someone. Tasting *her*.

The thought made her knees melt again.

So what now? Was he going to make her drop the towel? Was he going to take her back into the shower with him? Was he going to forget the shower completely and tumble her onto the bed? From the look on his face, all three were distinct options.

She wanted to run—to him and from him at the same time.

'Cyn.' Was it her imagination, or had his voice dropped a few tones? Slightly husky. Sexy. Turned on. 'Which side of the bed do you want?' he asked.

The one you're on.

Nope, she couldn't say that. She tried aiming for cool and sophisticated. 'Whatever.'

Brilliant! She sounded as if sharing a bed with a man she barely knew was something she'd done so many times before, not something that frightened the hell out of her.

'I usually sleep on the left,' he said.

Ouch. She'd let herself forget that this was a man who was used to sharing his bed. With lots of different women. And if he gave them come-to-bed looks like the one he was giving her right now, it was hardly surprising.

'Whatever,' she said again, faking nonchalance.

Concentrating on every step—please, please don't let her fall flat on her face in front of him—she walked over to the bed. The one thing she couldn't do was to drop her towel in front of him. She couldn't get into bed wearing the towel, either; that would make her look like a frightened virgin. She'd stopped being a virgin during her first year at university, but she wasn't even going to think about the frightened bit.

'Would you mind turning away?' she asked.

'Sure.'

To her relief, Max did the gentlemanly thing. Just in case he *was* tempted to peek, she turned her back. And dropped the towel.

CHAPTER FIVE

THE only thing was, turning his back meant Max could see Cyn's reflection. And what he saw was curves. Soft and full and just waiting for him to explore them. His fingertips tingled at the idea of touching her, learning the texture of her skin. And his mouth tingled even more at the idea of finding out exactly how her skin tasted.

But no way would he force her into doing anything she didn't want to do. He wasn't that type of guy. All the same, he knew how fragile his self-control was going to be. So he made sure that his shower was tepid, and then cold. And very, very long. And to spare Cyn's embarrassment he wrapped a towel round his hips before walking back into the bedroom.

She'd already turned her lamp off. He did the same before dropping his towel and climbing into bed.

The body beside him was absolutely rigid. Tension was coming off her in waves. Did she think he expected her to have sex with him, or something?

He wanted to—especially after he'd discovered that her curves were exactly as he'd guessed they'd be. But she was clearly scared. She'd responded to him on the dance floor, but that had been safe…in public, where he wouldn't have gone too far.

Lisa's words echoed in his head—*you don't have a hope in hell of getting past her defences anyway*—and he sighed. 'Relax, Cyn. I'm not going to make any demands on you.' Even though he wanted to.

'Sorry,' she mumbled back.

He was half tempted to put the light on again, so she could see for herself that he was being sincere. But he'd heard that little noise of relief she'd made when he'd switched the light off. Cyn was embarrassed. Big time. She wouldn't appreciate him seeing that embarrassment for himself.

What he didn't understand was *why* she felt embarrassed. Just as he was working out how to ask her without making her feel even more awkward and self-conscious, she broke the silence again. 'Max? We need to talk.'

Uh-oh. He didn't like the sound of this.

'It's a bit…well…delicate.'

That sounded even more worrying. Now he was nearly as tense as the woman lying beside him. 'What is?' he asked carefully.

'Tonight. The cost of the room, and all of that. I'll reimburse you.'

She'd *what*? Stunned, he said nothing.

'I don't expect you to pay for this. It's not part of the deal.'

'Deal?'

'Being Trophy Boyfriend for the night. We weren't supposed to be staying over. So it's my bill, okay?'

'It's not a problem, Cyn. Forget it and go to sleep.'

Except she couldn't. She couldn't stop worrying about things. 'I'm sorry,' she muttered.

'What for?'

'Everything. Dragging you here, your car getting crunched…'

'It wasn't all bad.' There was a pause. 'You did a great Baby.'

'Baby?'

He hummed 'I've Had The Time of My Life', and she suddenly twigged. Baby, as in Baby Houseman, the character who'd danced with Patrick Swayze's in *Dirty Dancing*. 'You did a pretty good Johnny Castle.'

'That's called teamwork.'

Yeah. And they'd made a brilliant team. They'd totally wiped the smugness off the faces of Michelle Wilson and her cronies. 'I'm still sorry about your car.'

'It'll mend.' He paused. 'Maybe I should make you be my chauffeur until it's fixed.'

Was that how he was planning to make her repay the favour she owed him? Fine. She could deal with that. 'All right. But I should warn you now, my car isn't in the same league as yours. It's small and practical.'

'Does it have a stereo?'

'Well, yeah.'

'Wheels and music. That's all I need. Though I'd want my CDs in the deck, not your girly stuff.'

Hang on. Was he being serious? Or was he teasing her? She couldn't tell. And she didn't dare put the light on so she could check his expression. Not when her face felt as if it were the colour and texture of a squashy, overripe tomato. 'Mmm-hmm,' she said carefully.

Silence.

'Cyn?'

'Yeah?'

'Relax.' She could hear laughter in his voice, now. 'I was teasing you. I'm not going to make you drive me around. I'm perfectly capable of getting a taxi if I need one. And London has a good public-transport system.'

'Sorry,' she mumbled. For a man who'd managed to

make her feel like a dancing queen for the first time in her life, he was very good at wrong-footing her.

'Cyn.'

'What?'

'Just stop worrying and go to sleep.'

How? How could she *possibly* go to sleep, with six feet of naked, drop-dead gorgeous male lying there next to her?

But, somehow, she did. And she surfaced the next morning feeling warm and comfortable and at peace with the world. Except… This didn't feel like her bed. And her face was virtually plastered to someone else's chest. A *male* chest.

The previous day snapped back into her head and she almost groaned aloud. Why couldn't she have stayed on her side of the bed instead of hogging his?

Though there was an even more pressing question. How the hell was she going to extract herself from this position without waking Max? Because their bodies were very, very tangled. She was lying on her left side, with her face buried in his chest and her head resting on his right arm.

Her face burned when she realised where her hands were. Her left hand was flat, sandwiched palm-down between his thighs, and her right hand was curved over his bottom. Possessively.

He was doing his share of the possessive bit, too. His right hand was resting on her shoulder, holding her close to him, and his left hand was curved over her hip.

It was intimate in the extreme. There was only one way they could possibly get closer…and her face burned even more at the thought. She really ought to move. Now.

But he was still asleep. At least, his breathing was deep and slow and regular. Unlike hers, which was fast and shallow.

One touch wouldn't hurt. One little touch—and then she'd wriggle out of his embrace. He wouldn't know a thing about it. One little touch…

She gave into temptation, and stroked the curve of his bottom.

Wow. She hadn't dared look, last night. The second she'd heard the bathroom door open, she'd closed her eyes tightly and turned her back to his side of the bed. She'd heard his towel hit the floor, but she hadn't dared to peek. Hadn't seen for herself if he looked as good out of the suit as he did in it. Or—her heart slammed harder against her ribs—as good as he'd looked half undressed.

He certainly *felt* good. Taut muscles, soft skin—the perfect combination. She couldn't resist gliding her fingertips along his gluteus maximus again. In tight jeans, she thought, Max Taylor would have women *fainting*.

He was an architect. Did that mean he sat behind a desk in a suit? Or did it mean he went on site dressed in a T-shirt, jeans, steel-capped boots and a hard hat? If it was the latter, she'd bet every woman whose office was in view of the sites he worked on would take a coffee break when he turned up—just so they could watch him.

And then she froze in horror. Because the hand resting on her hip moved. Just one finger. A slow, deliberate movement. Echoing what she'd just done to him, on a smaller patch of skin.

Max had just stroked her naked skin.

She couldn't breathe. Panic oozed from every pore. He was supposed to be asleep. No way could her touch have woken him. She hadn't squeezed, hadn't pressed hard. Just the lightest, softest glide of her fingertips against his skin.

Maybe he'd been awake all along. Just waiting to see what she would do.

Oh, God. What she *should* have done was to creep out of bed and get showered and dressed without waking him, then leave him a note to say she'd see him at breakfast. But no. She'd had to touch him. Stroke him. *Incite* him.

And now she was faced with one awake, aroused male. Literally facing him. Because her face was still pressed against his hard chest. And other parts of his body weren't shy in telling her that they were awake.

Worse, her own body was responding to the signals. Her breasts felt heavy, and she knew he'd feel her nipples pressing against his chest. He'd know that she was turned on, too.

This was bad!

'Good morning,' he said softly.

Say it. Come on. It's not that difficult, she told herself. Two little words. *Say it.* 'Good morning.'

Nope. She hadn't said it. She'd squeaked it. How embarrassing could she get?

The hand resting on her hip explored a little more.

'Your skin's so soft.' His voice was like a purr.

She couldn't make a coherent response. Not when he'd shifted slightly and pushed one leg between hers.

'Cyn.' His lips touched her forehead. Lightly, playfully. And her skin felt as if it had been burned.

She panicked. This couldn't be happening. They couldn't make love. They hardly knew each other. She hadn't cleaned her teeth. Her hair was a mess. Thank goodness the curtains were thick and it was still too dark for him to see her properly. There were a million and one reasons why she should stop this right now.

But he was stroking her skin. Nuzzling his mouth against her face. She couldn't think straight.

'Cinnamon,' he whispered, his breath fanning her ear. 'Your name makes me think of cinnamon. Cinnamon and apple pie. Cinnamon rolls. And I'm hungry.'

That was her get-out. They had to be downstairs for breakfast. Come *on*, mouth, open! Tell him we have to stop. Tell him we have to—

He stroked her skin again and she stopped thinking at all.

'I'm so hungry for you,' he told her, his voice husky. His hand skimmed up over her bottom. The curve of her waist. The soft swell of her belly.

When Lisa had played fairy godmother, why hadn't she magicked Cyn a washboard stomach as well?

Then again, midnight was long, long gone. They were back to pumpkins and mice.

But Max was still touching her. Still nuzzling her skin. Giving her tiny, cherishing, tempting kisses. Urging her to kiss him back.

She shouldn't be doing this.

And she couldn't help herself.

His hand drifted higher and skated over her ribcage. So near, so near—she ached for him to touch her properly, and a little moan slipped out: a little do-it-now-because-I-can't-hold-on moan.

He cupped her breast, and she gasped, tipping her head back and lifting her ribcage slightly. Offering herself to him.

He made a murmur of satisfaction, and his thumb rubbed against her nipple. This time, when she let out a sigh of need, he shifted so that his mouth could track down the sensitive bit at the side of her neck, then over her collar-bones.

Her common sense went completely walkabout. She wanted him, and she wanted him *right now*.

Stunning. Simply stunning. It was the only way Max could describe the way she felt. All soft, warm, womanly curves. Yesterday, he'd wanted to unwrap her. Today, he could.

Definitely birthday and Christmas and passing-his-driving-test-day all rolled into one—and then some.

She was so responsive. He couldn't help teasing her. He nuzzled her skin, breathing in her scent, revelling at the soft warmth against his face. He'd thought yesterday that her curves were lush. Now he knew just how lush, and they thrilled him even more.

Forget the fact that he was supposed to be looking after her. Right here, right now, they were just man and woman, wanting each other. And there was no reason why they had to stop; no commitments elsewhere.

One perfect day. Twenty-four hours. Starting from when he'd parked outside her house yesterday morning and discovered that the shy, workaholic geek he'd been expecting had morphed into something much, much more. Fast-forward to the way she'd danced with him, her body moving perfectly against his.

This time, her body would be moving *around* his. And, he thought as he trailed a line of kisses between her breasts, he was going to drown in delight. It was still dark outside, but the curtains were thick enough that they wouldn't have let any light through anyway. So he couldn't see her, though the rest of his senses were more than making up for it.

She arched up towards him and slid her hands into his hair, pulling him to her. He smiled against her skin. Impatient? He teased her a little more—just to prove that he had some self-control—and then did what he'd wanted to do since he'd seen her in the mirror, the previous night. He drew the tip of his tongue round her areola, then blew on the damp skin.

Her little 'oh' of surprised pleasure gave him such a kick. He didn't think Cyn was a virgin—but clearly the men in her previous relationships hadn't bothered to check that she was enjoying herself as much as they were. So this might just be the best way to end a perfect interlude. For both of them.

He scraped his teeth very gently across her nipple. She moaned; then, when he drew it into his mouth and sucked, she arched against him.

Good. But he could make it better still.

He switched his attention to her other breast. Her hands tangled in his hair, urging him on. This felt good, so good. He nuzzled his way lower, tracing the line of her ribcage with the tip of his nose and circling her navel with the tip of his tongue. Teasing her, arousing her, drawing out her anticipation until she was at the point of spontaneous combustion. He wanted her to flare for him. Magnesium, burning bright. He wanted her to see stars.

She tilted her hips, her thighs parting, and he stroked his way along her soft flesh. This was starting to be torture. He wasn't sure how much longer he could take it, either. He needed to feel her body wrapped round him. Now.

'Yes,' she whispered huskily as his fingers cupped her.

He could feel her pulse beating against him, and her skin was almost sizzling to the touch. His own was in pretty much the same state, and he was fairly sure that more than a few of his brain cells had fried the second he'd touched her.

'Cyn,' he murmured, and pushed one finger inside.

This time, her 'oh' of pleasure was long drawn out. She moved against him, clearly wanting more.

Just as he did.

He couldn't wait another second.

He knelt between her thighs, but when he was one millimetre from entering her, Cyn choked out his name.

He paused. 'What's wrong, honey?'

'Condom.'

The word stopped him in his tracks. Oh, Lord. What *had* he been thinking?

Well, he knew what he'd been thinking. He'd been so desperate to touch and taste Cyn, so desperate to be inside her, he'd been thinking about nothing else.

He certainly hadn't been thinking about being responsible.

He took a shuddering breath. 'I haven't got one.' He swallowed hard. 'Have you?'

'No.' Her voice was a whisper. A quiver of misery. 'Don't all men carry them?'

'No. Not all the time.' Only when he planned to make love. Which he hadn't, yesterday. 'I wasn't intending this to happen. So, no.'

And, without a condom, sex wasn't a good idea. Apart from the health risks, there were other potential consequences. Such as nine months from now.

He didn't do long-term relationships. Not since Gina. Nothing serious, nothing that lasted for more than three dates. No matter what women said at the beginning of a relationship, eventually they expected to come first. And it wouldn't happen with him. His job came first. Always would. He wasn't going to make promises he couldn't keep. No for evers; no 'Hey, let's settle down and start a family.' It wasn't him. He was an architect first, last and foremost. The only babies in his life were made out of ancient bricks and needed very, very careful handling to restore them to their former beauty.

So there was only one thing he could do.

Back off.

Gently, he shifted to lie on his back beside her. Give him a few minutes, and his body would settle down again. His mind would snap into place. And then they could deal with it.

She began shuffling away from him. 'I'd better get up.'

Her voice was thick with disappointment. Hell. It must feel as bad for her as it did for him. The touching. The teasing. The anticipation—and now the anticlimax, that sinking disappointment as their bodies realised they wouldn't get the release they craved. All because he hadn't expected this to happen. Because he hadn't been prepared. Because, despite the fact that he dated a lot, he didn't automatically assume that every date would end in bed. So he didn't carry condoms.

Well, there was something he could do. Something that would make them both feel better. Stop the ache. He reached out and grabbed her hand. 'Don't go.'

'I...'

'Cyn. I know we're both being sensible. That we can't do what we both want to do. But there's something we *can* do. Something almost as good.' Something that would definitely ease the ache.

'What?'

'Let me touch you,' he said softly. 'Let me taste you.'

He felt the shiver of desire run through her, and smiled. Oh, yeah. This was going to be all right, after all. He pulled her back into his arms and kissed her. A deep, intense kiss that promised everything would be fine. And then he got to explore his way down her body again: her neck, the hollows of her collar-bones, the curve of her elbow, the soft, sweet-tasting skin just under her breasts, the hourglass curve of her waist. Touching and tasting. Her hands were back in his hair again, and she was moving restlessly underneath him, rocking her hips, making tiny impatient moans.

He took pity on her, and slid his hand back between her thighs. The first touch had her trembling. The second had her sighing. And then he replaced his hand with his mouth, and the result was a guttural, incoherent moan. She shuddered, and fell apart in his arms.

Wow. He'd never had a reaction that strong before. It made him feel like the king of the universe. The fact that he could reduce this clever, capable woman to a pile of mush… Amazing.

He shifted to lie beside her again, pillowing her head on his chest. Weirdly, he felt content. Not frustrated— even though he was still aroused and he knew there was no chance he'd be able to do what he really wanted and sink into her soft, heated sex. He was just content. And Cyn…Cyn was still stunned into silence.

She curled against him, her hand flat against his stomach. And then he realised that her hand was moving. Downwards. It looked as if she was planning to return the favour.

He gasped as her fingers circled him.

'Cyn. You don't have to.'

She kissed his chest. 'I know.'

'It's not… I don't expect…' When she was kissing her way down his ribcage like that, no way could he string a sentence together. He couldn't even think one, let alone say it.

Her hair brushed against his abdomen, and he shivered. Oh, Lord. He tried again. Made a real effort, even managed to sound a lot more coherent than he actually felt. 'Don't feel you have to do anything. You're under no ob—'

And the rest of the word was lost as her beautiful mouth did what he'd wanted it to do, since the moment he'd set eyes on her yesterday morning: it wrapped itself round him.

CHAPTER SIX

'YOU are the biggest jerk in the world,' Max told himself silently when the spray from the shower had beaten some common sense back into his brain. 'You took advantage of her. Lisa told you Cyn's a shy workaholic and needs protecting. Lisa told you you'd never get through her defences. So what do you do? You grab her.'

Though, to be fair, he *had* been provoked. She'd been the first one to start touching; he'd merely reacted. And he had told her she was under no obligation to do the same for him—well, he'd tried to tell her. Just his mouth and his brain hadn't been working in sync.

They were working in sync now. And he hated himself for it. How was he going to face her now? What was she expecting from him?

In his experience, women wanted 'for ever'. That was what Gina had wanted. She'd had their whole future mapped out: a fairy-tale wedding with a princess dress and a horse and carriage, a baby conceived on their wedding night in a four-poster bed on a tropical island, another baby two years later, a dog, a cat, a pony and a hamster, and probably another two children. Two girls, two boys. Nice and neat. Oh, and a pretty four-bedroomed cottage with roses round the door, in the village where her parents lived.

Her dream. Her parents' dream. His parents' dream. Everyone's dream…except his.

Max had tried to go along with it. He'd really, really tried, even though inside he'd been panicking that he wasn't ready for that depth of commitment, that he still had journeys to make and dreams to fulfil before he settled down.

And then the chance had fallen into his lap. The chance to head up the restoration department for an architectural practice in London—the job he'd been waiting for all his life. It had meant he'd get to work on some truly amazing buildings. To feel he was doing something important, something that really mattered. Something that would last for longer than his own lifetime. Something that made him feel alive.

Except it had also meant moving to London. Working long hours. Putting his job first.

Gina hadn't wanted to move to London. She hadn't wanted him to commute or be a weekend husband, either. She definitely hadn't wanted to give him a year or so to live his dream first before he settled down to fatherhood.

It had ended in tears, on both sides. He'd loved Gina—or had thought he loved her—but he'd discovered that he hadn't loved her enough. So he'd taken the job instead of marrying her and settling down.

Which made him a selfish bastard.

It was why he didn't date any more; he knew he was a selfish bastard and would always put his job first. Hell, he even had his own practice, now, so he was a million times worse than when he'd worked for someone else—he no longer had a manager to point out that he was putting in too many hours and needed to get a life outside. He didn't *want* a life outside; he loved his buildings.

And he'd just proved his selfishness all over again. He'd taken advantage of Cyn. Had a one-night stand with her—well, a one-morning stand—when he never, but never, did one-night-or-morning stands. Didn't do relationships any more, apart from business ones.

How on earth was he going to sort this out?

In the bedroom, Cyn was putting the finishing touches to her make-up. Not as professional a job as Lisa had made of it, but it was passable.

Though, right now, she could have done with the old caked-on stuff she'd always hated. Something that would mask her face, hide her expression from Max.

How was she going to face him again?

He'd been nice, let her shower first. But she'd noticed how he'd avoided looking at her when she'd walked out of the bathroom, fully dressed. She knew exactly what he was thinking: she'd thrown herself at him, therefore she was desperate, and she expected him to turn this embarrassing mess into a proper relationship.

Worse, he might even think this had been a set-up in the first place.

What a fiasco. How the hell was she going to explain it to Lisa? *I jumped your boss's bones. Um, better start looking for another job, my friend. Sorry.*

No, that wouldn't do at all.

She took a deep breath. It could have been worse. At least she'd thought about a condom *before* it was too late. She hadn't repeated her mother's mistake. Though it sure as hell felt like it. She didn't do one-night stands, and the only commitment she planned to make in the immediate—or even foreseeable—future was to her job. In her experience, men weren't big on commitment anyway. Her father certainly hadn't been. And she wasn't expecting Max to declare undying love and ask her to marry him.

It had been sex, that was all.

Good sex. *Very* good sex. As far as they'd gone.

No. She wasn't going to think about that. What it would feel like when he entered her. How his body would fit with hers.

Because it wasn't going to happen. No commitment.

So there was nothing for it. She'd have to bite the bullet.

The minute he opened the bathroom door, she said, 'About this morning—'

At exactly the same time as he said, 'About this morning—'

They both stopped.

'After you,' she said.

'Ladies first,' he countered.

She took a deep breath. 'I don't want you to get the wrong idea about me. I don't do this sort of thing. I don't know why…' Liar. She *did* know why. There was something about him that made her hormones sit up and beg. Big time. So Cyn Reynolds—the woman who had such a 'planner's cup' in her psychometric test results that the human resources department had actually photocopied it and pinned it on the wall—had acted on impulse for almost the first time in her life.

And even thinking about what they'd done together was sending trickles of desire through her veins. She had to shut them down. Fast. 'I… Look, can we just go down to breakfast? I need coffee.' And a sugar rush. Flaky, buttery croissants topped with strawberry jam.

Though that made her think of something really bad. Of Max Taylor licking the buttery crumbs from her fingers. Of his mouth sucking against her skin. Of…

Oh, she needed that coffee. *Now*.

Max wished he'd gone first, now. Explained that he didn't do long term. Explained that she was lovely, beautiful, clever—all the other things he knew women wanted to hear—but it was just *him*. He wasn't looking for permanent.

This morning shouldn't have happened. Wouldn't happen again. But he couldn't change the past, so there was no point in beating himself up about it.

He just wished he didn't feel so damned *guilty* about it.

At least breakfast would give them some space.

Except it didn't. Neither of them knew where to look, Cyn spilled her coffee all over the tablecloth, and Max was trying very hard not to watch her eating toast and honey because her mouth was just too tempting. There was a smear of honey on her lower lip and he itched to lean over and lick it off. Which was bad. He wasn't going to get involved. Been there, done that, and mopped up the disaster afterwards. Never again.

At least the recovery company was on time. His beautiful—crunched—car was hitched to the back of the tow truck. And a quiet word with the driver ensured that he'd break the rules and drop Cyn home before taking Max and the car to the repair shop.

Going back to London couldn't have been more different from their journey out, Cyn thought. On the way to the wedding, she'd been nervous, but at least they'd been talking. She'd been dressed to kill. They'd had good music on the stereo, something she'd been able to sing along to.

On the way home, there was nothing to say. Her clothes were looking crumpled. She might just as well have a tattoo on her forehead saying, 'Pity me, I'm desperate'. And as for the music: the tow-truck driver had chosen a country and western station. Not her taste at all, but she didn't want to make a fuss. Particularly as Max wasn't saying anything, either.

How could time stretch like this? Every time she glanced at her watch, she was sure that whole minutes had passed. But no. Just a second or two.

It seemed like for ever, but then the tow truck pulled up outside her house.

Last night, Max had said that the recovery company would only make one stop: the coach works. How…? The question must have been written on her face, because Max said, *sotto voce*, 'I asked nicely.'

'Right. Um, thank you.' All her instincts were screaming at her to run—to wrench open the truck door, sprint down the path, and slam her front door safely behind her. But she'd been brought up properly. 'Would you like to come in for coffee?'

He smiled. A smile that looked suspiciously professional to her—she'd bet he'd learned to fake it when dealing with difficult clients. Just as she did. 'Thanks, but I have to go with the car.'

It was true—but she could guess what lay behind his smile. Relief. He had the perfect excuse to leave.

Well, that was good. Because now she could go indoors, face Lisa and tell her housemate what a horrible mess she'd made of everything.

'Well, thank you for…' *Everything.* The word stuck in her throat. No. she wasn't going to make this worse by saying something he could misinterpret. 'Thank you for coming to the wedding with me. I appreciate it.'

'Any time.'

Meaning: Thank God, it's all over and we never have to see each other again. Okay. She could deal with that.

'And I'm sorry about the car.'

He shrugged. 'These things happen.'

She climbed out of the tow truck. 'Bye.' She wasn't

going to embarrass them both with, 'See you.' Because they wouldn't see each other again. Which was a good thing...wasn't it?

Cyn noted that he waited until she'd unlocked the front door before letting the truck drive off. Max's courtesy and manners were impeccable. So were hers—and, because he'd refused to let her pay even her share of the hotel room, the least she could do was send him something to say thank you. She knew he loved music, but she couldn't send him concert tickets—he might think she was fishing for a date, or feel obliged to ask her along. Flowers were out, too—women appreciated them and men didn't. A plant for his office? No, that was too much like sending him something he'd have to pass every day and think of her. Ick.

She flicked through her favourite Internet shops, and smiled. Yeah! Handmade chocolates. Hadn't Max himself said that he'd love to have a chocolatier for a client, especially if he got to try new flavours? Within five minutes, Cyn had placed her order, checked Max's office address on the Internet, typed in a suitable thank-you note to go with the delivery—the Gold Service so the chocolates would hit his desk by courier tomorrow morning—and paid for it.

Done and dusted.

They'd never have to cross each other's paths again.

CHAPTER SEVEN

MAX sifted through his post. Another 'Sorry, I've changed my mind' letter. Sure, it was part of business—you didn't get every job you tendered for—but it didn't happen to him very often. Where he was concerned, it usually happened when a client's circumstances changed, or if there was a particularly time-consuming difficulty with planning and the client decided it wasn't worth going ahead. But this was the third loss in a month, and *that* wasn't normal. Something was going on…but what?

He knew he had a solid reputation. He wasn't the cheapest architect, but he wasn't the most expensive either. And he lived by the rule of underpromising and overde-livering—which meant he always delighted his clients. So why was he losing tenders now?

It had all started with Phil Watkins—who had gone on to use a design very, very similar to the one Max had produced. Different enough for Max not to be able to take legal action. But still similar enough to make him wonder.

He buzzed through to Lisa. 'Call me paranoid,' he said, 'but can you run me off a list of people who've changed their mind in the last year?'

'Sure. What's happened?' she asked.

'That's what I'm trying to find out,' Max said.

A few minutes later, she walked in with a mug of coffee, a couple of sheets of paper and a box.

'Here,' she said.

'What's this?' Max asked, glancing at the box.

'Just came by courier.'

He opened it. Exclusive handmade chocolates. The type he particularly liked. He smiled. 'Hey. Maybe today isn't going to be quite as bad as I thought.'

Lisa's eyes widened. 'You're not going to eat them all at once?'

'Watch me,' he said dryly. 'Actually, you'd better grab a couple now. While there are some left.'

She grinned. 'It's supposed to be women who reach for chocolate when they're stressed.'

Max grinned back. 'Honey, women don't have a monopoly on something this good.' His smile faded. 'And I'm not stressed.' Not yet. Just…suspicious. And he was checking out a hunch.

Then he read the card that came with it. 'Thanks for escorting me. Best, Cyn.' Very cool and calm.

Hmm. He could remember her being distinctly hot and bothered. In the nicest way.

'So who are they from?' Lisa asked.

'Grateful client.' Not a complete lie. It had been a job, of sorts. Just not one in his usual line of work. He offered the box to Lisa, though he was careful not to show her the card. 'I might need you to make a few phone calls this morning, when I've worked through this list.'

He must have sounded worried—or she was just in super-PA mode and had tuned in to the way his mind worked, because she picked it up straight away. 'What's going on, Max?'

'Right now, I'm not sure,' he admitted. 'I think someone might be trying to poach my client list.'

'What—but, why? Who?'

'I don't know who or why or how. But I need to find out and stop it before there's serious damage.'

She bit her lip. 'Bad enough to…?'

To bring his business crashing down and put her out of a job? 'Not if I can find out what's going on.'

She nodded. 'Okay, boss. Just let me know what I can do.'

'For now, it's business as usual,' Max said. 'Oh—and I need Cyn's work number, when you've got a minute.'

One eyebrow arched. 'Cyn's?'

'Mmm-hmm. Business.'

Lisa gave him a look that said she didn't believe a word of it, but took a pencil from his desk and scribbled Cyn's number on a sticky note. 'She's usually in wall-to-wall meetings on Monday mornings, so you'll probably get her voicemail. I've given you her email address as well.'

'Thanks.' He'd call Cyn later. Just to thank her for the chocolates. Once he'd got more of an idea about what the hell was going on with his client list.

Karl walked into the meeting room and glanced at Cyn.

Then he stopped dead and looked again. 'Cyn?'

'Yes?'

He smiled and sat down. 'Hi, how are you?'

It was the most attention Karl, the marketing manager at RCS, had ever paid her. Usually, he smiled politely and pretty much ignored the quiet woman in the grey suit. But, over the weekend, Lisa had whisked away Cyn's usual wardrobe and this morning had insisted that her new look of the weekend should continue into her work life. And clearly how Cyn looked mattered more than what she could do, because Karl was the fourth male colleague in a row today who'd noticed the change and suddenly paid her a lot more attention.

And that *really* rankled.

'I'm fine, thank you,' Cyn said politely.

'Nice weekend?'

'Um, yes. And you?'

'Fine.' He smiled at her. A real killer smile. Half the women in the office mooned over Karl Fiennes, with his blond good looks and cornflower blue eyes. Half the women in the office would want to murder her, for getting this much attention from him.

'Are you busy at lunchtime?'

Was he asking her out? Oh, get real! He meant he needed to squeeze in an extra business meeting. 'Um, I'll check,' she said, and fiddled with her PDA. 'I can fit you in at half past one for about twenty minutes.' She could always ask one of her team to bring her a sandwich and an espresso on their way back from lunch. 'Which client are we talking about?'

'We're not. I was asking you to have lunch with me,' Karl said, giving her another of those killer smiles.

'Oh. I, um…' Tail-spin. She hadn't expected this. She shook herself mentally. 'Sorry, I don't really have time for a lunch-break today.'

'Tomorrow, then? Or maybe dinner tonight?'

'I… Er…' To her relief, the rest of the team came into the meeting, so she was saved having to answer. Dinner with Karl Fiennes? A week ago, she would probably have said yes. Well, after a bit of prodding from Lisa—Cyn really wasn't that bothered about looking for Mr Right. Her career was more important to her. The only problem was, since the weekend, she'd had someone else in her head…someone with dark hair, not blond…someone with slate-blue eyes and the sexiest smile ever…

Except Max had made it clear he wasn't interested in taking their relationship further. He hadn't even responded to the chocolates she'd sent him—well, not that she'd expected much. Just an email or something to say he'd got them. And she definitely wasn't going to make her mother's mistake and eat her heart out, waiting for someone who didn't really want her. So maybe she should go out with Karl. He wasn't the serious type—but she wasn't looking for that kind of relationship anyway.

She just had to put Max Taylor out of her mind.

She managed it through the entire meeting. But then it was over, and Karl was at her side again. 'So are we on for dinner tonight?'

'I...I'm a bit tied up with work,' she prevaricated. 'There's that art gallery launch on Friday—the Wharf Gallery in Docklands. One of my team said something about a bug in the video installation systems—it needs fixing before the launch. And I'm managing the project, so I want to have a look at what's going on.'

Karl nodded, as if understanding. 'Tell you what—why don't we go to the launch party together? As the marketing manager, I should be there. You're the project manager and lead programmer, so you really ought to be there too.'

'In case of last-minute glitches that need fixing,' Cyn agreed. 'You know what touch screens are like. Temperamental.'

'No, I meant so you get your share of the glory—the backroom boys are always underappreciated.' Karl smiled.

Backroom *boys*. Hmm. She wasn't a boy, thank you very much.

Not that he'd noticed her narrowed gaze, because he continued, 'And I live quite near you, don't I? So it makes sense that we share a taxi.'

He didn't give her the chance to say no. And it *was* work-related. So it didn't quite count as a date. Not that she should be worrying about two-timing Max. She wasn't going out with him anyway, was she? One unexpected night together did not a relationship make. 'Okay,' she replied.

'Good. I'll catch you later and we'll sort out the details.' Karl gave her a slow, sexy wink. *'Ciao, bella.'*

He was talking Italian to her, now?

Last week she'd been everyone's favourite geek. The one everyone rang when they were in a flap and needed something fixed fast, and then invited her to the pub afterwards as part of the crowd. This week, she had men winking at her, asking her out to dinner—one on one— and speaking to her in Italian.

Maybe Lisa was right. She should have ditched the grey suits years ago.

By the time Max finished working through his list, he was seriously perplexed. One of the clients hadn't gone ahead because of a change in circumstances. Another had had a huge row with the planning department and had cancelled all the plans in a fit of pique—which had probably been a lucky escape for him, Max thought, because he could do without the kind of clients who insisted on overseeing everything rather than trusting to a professional's expertise. And there had been no further planning notices for those particular properties, so he knew the jobs hadn't gone elsewhere. He could tick those off his list.

Three clients had said they were going with another architect who'd tendered; one of those cited cost and the other two cited design. Planning permission had been granted for those three; he made a note to check who the contractor was and who had done the final designs. Maybe there would be a common factor.

The three who'd cancelled in the past month all just said

they'd changed their mind. One, he could accept. Three was too much of a coincidence. Particularly when the planning permission was still outstanding—the requests hadn't been withdrawn. So although they'd said they'd changed their mind, they were still intending to go ahead. Just with someone else rather than him.

It looked as if someone was trying to cut in on his business. But who? Why?

Max couldn't remember any business disputes with a client, or a contractor or a supplier. He didn't tender at low prices and bring in the final job at a much higher rate; he always met his deadlines; he was clear and direct about his plans; and although he'd heard rumours of corruption he'd never been asked for a backhander to get planning permission or building regulations through.

An ex making trouble, maybe? He couldn't see it. According to his mum, Gina was happily married with the second of her much-wanted babies on the way. And his past girlfriends…well, they'd all known the score right from the outset and accepted it. At least, they'd told *him* they accepted it, and he'd had no reason to think otherwise.

When Lisa came back from lunch, he'd ask her to do a little schmoozing. See if she could pick up anything on the grapevine.

Then he realised he'd eaten well over half the chocolates. And he still hadn't phoned Cyn to thank her for them. She might be at lunch; on the other hand, Lisa claimed Cyn was a workaholic. Maybe she worked through lunch, ate a sandwich at her desk.

Only one way to find out. He dialled the number Lisa had scribbled on the sticky note.

'Cyn Reynolds' phone.'

Max straightened in his chair. He hadn't been expecting a man to answer her phone. Probably a colleague.

Most techies were male, weren't they? 'Hi. Is Cyn there, please?'

'She's not at her desk at the moment. Can anyone else help, or can I take a message?'

'Could you ask her to ring me, please? Max Taylor.' He gave his direct line number.

'Will she know which project it's concerning?'

'It's personal,' Max said.

'Personal?' The voice sharpened. 'She hasn't mentioned anyone called Max to me.'

Who did this guy think he was—her keeper? 'And you are?'

'Karl Fiennes.'

'Her secretary?' Max guessed.

'Hardly.' Scornful. 'I'm the marketing manager.'

Marketing manager? So what the hell was *he* doing answering Cyn's phone? She was a techie—she had nothing to do with marketing!

As if Max had spoken aloud, Karl said, 'I was waiting to take her to lunch.'

'I see,' Max said. Maybe it was a business lunch—they were going to discuss one of Cyn's projects and this was the only time she could make today. No, it had to be business. Otherwise Cyn wouldn't have needed Max to play Trophy Boyfriend at the wedding. This Karl Fiennes could have done it, couldn't he? 'Perhaps you'd be good enough to tell her I called.'

'Sure.'

A little too greasy for Max's liking. And when Cyn hadn't returned his call by four o'clock, Max surmised that Mr Oily hadn't passed the message on.

Great. Another cloud to rain on his day. As if this particular Monday hadn't been bad enough already. Might as well finish it in style and get the brush-off from the woman herself.

He dialled Cyn's work number again. And this time she answered her phone herself.

'Good afternoon, Cyn Reynolds speaking.'

'Hi. It's Max.'

'Oh! Hi.'

She sounded a little flustered, he thought. So had this Karl guy given her his message, or not? 'I'm ringing to thank you for the chocolates. They were spectacular.'

'Were? You mean, Lisa annexed half of them?'

'No. It's been one of those days,' Max admitted ruefully. 'But the chocolates were a bright spot.'

'Good.'

'I also need a favour.'

'A favour?' There was a distinctly worried note in her voice.

'Escort duty. At an artsy party. I have to schmooze a potential client.' And, until he'd found out who was trying to sink his business, Max couldn't afford to reject potential clients out of hand. 'Apparently, Mr Harris prefers to work with men who are *attached*. He thinks they're more stable than bachelors.'

'That's discrimination,' Cyn pointed out.

'I know, but he's the client. What he wants, he gets. So I need a trophy girlfriend for the evening.' He coughed. 'And, as I did it for you…'

'I owe you, so you're collecting.'

'Got it in one.' Max wasn't going to admit to himself just how much of a pleasure it would be to collect this particular favour.

'Okay.' She sounded slightly unsure. 'When is it?'

'Friday night.'

'*This* Friday?'

'Yes.'

'Ah. Sorry. I'm, um, already booked.'

'Work?'

'Sort of. It's the launch party for one of my clients.'

'Any chance you could do both in one evening?'

'Maybe if I was going on my own, but I'm with Karl. I can't.'

Karl? Mr Oily? Did she mean she was going to the party with Karl on a work basis—as colleagues—or that she was *with* Karl, as in, she was his girlfriend?

No. He remembered the way she'd reacted to him on Sunday morning. Cyn Reynolds wasn't the kind of girl to hop from his bed straight into another man's. Karl was a colleague. Being one of the marketing glamour boys, he'd probably bulldozed Cyn into going with him—and no doubt he'd leave her to do all the hard work while he lapped up all the plaudits.

'Well, looks as if I'll be schmoozing on my own, then.' Not that Max really wanted to go to a gallery launch. Maybe he'd just forget it. 'Pity.'

'I'm sorry.'

'It probably would have bored you stupid anyway. It's at a new art gallery in Docklands.'

There was a pause. 'Not the Wharf Gallery?'

'How did you know?'

She coughed. 'Friday's their launch party.'

He made the connection instantly. 'They're your client? But…they're an art gallery. You're an IT specialist.' Since when did the two mix?

'They have some very specialist IT requirements. Including touch screen terminals to showcase some of their clients' work.'

'Uh-huh.' But the important thing was, they were going to the same party. Friday—which had been something he hadn't been in the mood for—suddenly held all kinds of possibilities. 'Well, it looks as if the problem's solved because we're going to be in the same place. I'll see you there, then.' And he'd get a chance to check out Mr Oily. 'Until Friday,' he said softly, and hung up before she could make an excuse.

CHAPTER EIGHT

CYN didn't get a chance to worry about the party because debugging, ordering replacement screens for the two defective ones, and solving minor glitches for the gallery project took up all her working time during the week—and a bit more besides. But while she was getting ready on Friday night, her misgivings returned in full.

After the week she'd had, she wasn't in the mood for going out. She wanted to chill out at home, in front of a good film, with a tub of her favourite ice cream. But she needed to see the job through—to stay for at least the first half of the launch party. Problem was, she was going there with Karl…and she was also meeting Max.

Awkward. *Very* awkward. But Karl was a colleague and Max was an acquaintance. Going to the party with Karl didn't mean that she couldn't talk to anyone else there, did it? And seeing Max…

Her pulse speeded up. Not good. She had to stay cool, calm and collected. Not think about last weekend. Not think about being in bed with Max Taylor. Not remember how his hands and his mouth had tipped her over the edge of pleasure. Max didn't do relationships, and she wasn't looking for one anyway, she reminded herself.

The doorbell rang, and she draped Lisa's black wrap round her shoulders before answering the door.

'Hi.'

Karl leaned against the wall and smiled at her. 'Wow. You look gorgeous.'

'Thank you.' Though she knew it was just marketing-man's flattery, it still made her feel good. *Gorgeous*. Much better than 'fine'.

'Ready?' he asked.

'Sure.' She locked her front door and allowed him to escort her to the taxi. She chatted with him about nothing much on the way there, but smothered a yawn as they reached the gallery reception. 'Sorry, Karl. I don't mean to be rude. I've pretty much had my nose to the grind-stone—and I might not make the end of the party,' she warned.

'No problem. We'll leave whenever you've had enough.'

Meaning what? That he expected to leave with her— come home with her—get to know her an awful lot better? She shook herself. Of course not. Karl was a player, but he wasn't stupid. Of course he knew she wanted to keep their relationship strictly business. Colleagues only. Didn't he? 'Hey. It's work, and I know you have to schmooze the client. I'll just slip away quietly.'

'No way. I'll see you safely home.'

It was the word 'safely' that did it. He was being nice, not being creepy, she decided. Which made her feel even more guilty for doubting him. She shook her head. 'We're there to represent RCS. You need to stay.'

Eventually, he nodded. 'All right, but only as long as you promise me you'll take a taxi.'

If it meant she could go home on her own with no hassle, she'd promise him almost anything. 'Sure.' Now for the crunch bit. She had to tell him about Max. There wasn't an easy way to say it. But she couldn't be too blunt about it. 'I expect you'll know a few people here tonight.'

'Probably,' Karl agreed.

'I think a friend of mine's going to be here. I, um, mentioned I was coming here with you. So he might want to catch up with me. If you don't mind.'

'Sure.'

Karl's smile looked ever so slightly forced. Surely he wasn't jealous?

'He?'

'Max Taylor,' Cyn explained. 'He knows Lisa.' And Karl knew Lisa from the time she'd temped at RCS.

'Right.'

Karl's smile was definitely forced, now. Though Cyn had no idea why. There was no reason why he would know Max.

'But you're here with *me* tonight,' Karl added.

Ouch. That sounded possessive. 'On behalf of RCS,' she reminded him. She'd seen tonight as work, right from the start. Hadn't he?

'Relax. It's a party,' Karl said.

Nope, it didn't sound as if he saw tonight as work. Somehow she was going to have to explain to him. Though she had a nasty feeling it was going to be easier said than done.

Mr Harris, one of the major patrons of the Wharf Gallery and the owner of a Docklands warehouse that was ripe for restoration, hadn't arrived yet. So far, Max had spent twenty-three minutes and forty-nine seconds wandering round the building and assessing it. The architect had made a reasonable job of converting the old warehouse, but there were a few original features missing. Features that Max would have showcased, lovingly restored—made *part* of the gallery.

You're meant to be in schmooze mode, not nit-picking other people's work, he reminded himself. Smile.

He pretended to be studying one of the installations and was about to accept a second glass of champagne when something made him turn round. And what he saw made him feel as if someone had just rabbit-punched him in the stomach. Hard.

Because Cyn had just walked through the door. Looking amazing, in a little black dress—and there was a man beside her, carefully taking the wrap from her shoulders.

He narrowed his eyes. So this was Karl.

It had only taken a few clicks of the mouse for Max to find Karl Fiennes on the RCS website and check out his profile. Marketing Manager. Ha! Max knew the breed: all charm and no substance, in his view. Karl was just like the rest of them—Max could tell from the photograph. Clearly the guy modelled himself on a certain Hollywood movie star. Blond good looks, very white teeth, charming smile. Tonight he was in a dinner jacket and cummerbund. As if he were escorting Cyn to the Oscars or something, instead of a business project. Pathetic. The guy wasn't in the same league as the film star, by a long way. And Max really disliked men who thought themselves gorgeous.

He'd hoped Cyn was only coming here with Karl on business. Though the hand resting lightly on Cyn's back definitely said, 'Mine'. The way Karl brushed a piece of lint from her dress screamed 'intimate'. And the quick little glances towards her were definitely those of a lover.

A *lover*.

Bile rose in Max's gut at the thought of Karl touching Cyn the same way *he'd* touched her. Part of him wanted to march over to the pair of them, sock Karl on the jaw, then hoist Cyn over his shoulder and march out of the party with his prize.

Except she'd be so embarrassed that she'd never speak to him again, let alone anything else.

But then she caught his eye. And his heart went straight into meltdown.

Cyn had forgotten just how gorgeous Max Taylor was. That perfect bone structure, those beautiful eyes, that sensuous mouth…a mouth that had kissed her all over…a mouth that had teased her to screaming pitch—and then taken her right over the edge.

She wanted to see him smile. Who was she trying to kid? She didn't want to see him smile. She wanted to see his eyes go glassy, the way they had when she'd repaid the compliment. She wanted to see his mouth parted in an 'oh' of pleasure. She wanted to see his hands curled into tight fists of bliss. She wanted to watch him lose control.

Tonight, he was dressed entirely in black; all he needed were little wire-rimmed spectacles and he'd be the epitome of an intellectual sex-god, the kind of man who could tempt Cyn out of her 'no relationships' rule. Particularly as she remembered exactly what he'd looked like wearing nothing but her. And she remembered exactly how he'd sounded, too. Little whimpers of pleasure, all the sweeter because she'd known he'd been trying to hold back, to keep some degree of control.

But then a group of people blocked her view of him. By the time they'd moved again, Max was gone.

Too late.

Disappointment swooped in her stomach. Then she stiffened her backbone. If Max Taylor really wanted to see her, he'd find her.

Until then, she had work to do.

Though, right now, her concentration was shot to pieces.

Karl Fiennes' body language said very clearly, 'She's mine'.

Max thought otherwise.

And Cyn herself didn't look that comfortable. Max knew she didn't like parties. Maybe she needed rescuing. He started to work his way through the crowded room towards her.

Then he saw Karl whispering in her ear. She nodded. And Max watched in dismay as Karl led her out onto one of the balconies. For hundreds of years, men had taken women onto balconies at parties with one thing in mind.

A kiss.

And it made Max want to punch a wall. *He* should be the one taking Cyn out to the balcony, not Mr Oily. *He* should be the one stealing a kiss. Because Cyn was most definitely his.

'It's pretty out here, isn't it?' Karl asked, nodding towards the lights reflected on the water.

'Yes.' It was pretty. And, better still, it was quieter than the party. The buzz of noise, people chatting and laughing and being luvvy, was giving Cyn a headache. The background music—something jazzy she didn't recognise—was pleasant enough, but she could barely hear it over the party hubbub.

She needed a breather—but she'd just made another mistake. A really stupid one. Because Karl had no doubt interpreted this as an invitation.

'Cyn.' His voice was soft, breathy. Expectant.

'Maybe we ought to go in. It's a bit chilly out here,' she said, hoping to forestall him.

He sighed. 'Why do I get the feeling that you're trying to give me the brush-off?'

'I…' Probably because she was. But nicely. She bit her lip. 'Karl, you're a really nice guy, and I find you very attractive.'

'But?'

Thank God! He was bright enough to read between her words. There was a but. An enormous but in neon lettering. 'We're too different.'

'Are we? We don't know each other that well, Cyn.'

True—but she knew enough to know she didn't want to take it further.

'We can have fun exploring our differences. Maybe we can learn new things from each other,' he suggested.

She could guess what 'new things' meant.

'Let's give it a try and see where it leads us,' he coaxed.

Into his bed, no doubt—in *his* mind.

He took her hand and kissed the palm—a gesture she'd just bet had women falling at his feet. Funny how it left her cold; she had to fight not to snatch her hand back.

Poor guy, it wasn't his fault.

He just wasn't Max.

'I… Karl, I'm flattered, I really am. But I just know that spark's not there between us,' she said quietly. Because she'd already met someone who made her feel that spark. A man who had the potential to make her want to put herself before her career. And she didn't want to repeat her mum's mistakes. Cyn already knew that relationships on the rebound didn't work.

Not that she wanted to explain it. Drag up old hurts, old failings. She'd moved on from that. 'I'm sorry,' she whispered.

Karl nodded. 'Okay. I'm sorry. I've pushed you too far, too fast. We'll take it slower.'

Slower? Um, no. She wanted a dead halt. 'Look, I'd better go check everything's all right—just in case there's been a last-minute glitch,' she said quickly. 'And then I might book a taxi and go home. I've got a bit of a headache. See you, um, later, maybe?'

'Sure,' he said, not looking in the slightest bit fazed.

She'd pin Lisa down over the weekend. Get some help on how to get the message across to Karl. And by Monday lunchtime he would be perfectly clear how things stood between them. Strictly business.

Her cheeks were pink. *Pink*. As if she'd just been kissed. Very thoroughly. Max ground his teeth. This was ridiculous. He had no claim over Cyn, so why was he feeling so ragingly jealous?

Max loosened his collar. He needed some air—to clear his head before he approached Cyn, who was determinedly making her way across the room; maybe she was on her way to the Ladies'? He was about to head for the patio when he noticed something. Karl was standing in the doorway that led out to the balcony—and from this angle it looked very much as if he was flirting. Flirting with another woman. Touching her, too—the little early courtship rituals of brushing lint off her clothes. Grooming.

And this was the man Cyn had chosen? A man who couldn't stop himself flirting and touching other women when his date had gone to the bathroom? No way. She deserved better. *Much* better.

Max caught himself clenching his fists, and deliberately stretched his fingers to relax his hands. Much as he would have liked to punch Karl on the nose for messing Cyn around, making a scene would do nothing except embarrass her. No, there was a better way of dealing with this. He'd warn the man off.

He strode over to the man in the doorway. 'Fiennes, isn't it?' he asked.

Karl's eyes narrowed slightly as he took in the other man's appearance and clearly noted that Max was a good two inches taller than he was. Karl was also obviously trying to look cool in front of the woman he'd just been flirting with. Fine. She might not be able to tell that his bow tie wasn't hand tied. And if that meant he'd leave Cyn alone, that was fine by Max. Very fine.

'I'm sorry. Have we met?' Karl queried.

'Not in person.' Max held his hand out. 'Taylor. Max Taylor.' He made his handshake deliberately firm. 'Thanks for looking after Cyn for me until I got here.'

Karl's eyes narrowed even more. 'Looking after her?'

'She's told me you're colleagues and that you'd keep an eye on her tonight. I appreciate that. She's not really one for parties.'

'I think there's been some mistake.' Karl drew himself up to his full—lesser—height. 'Cyn came here tonight with me.'

'On business.'

Karl shook his head. 'No. I mean *with* me.'

Max smiled. 'I don't think so. Because I'm sure you wouldn't be so sleazy as to chat up another woman while your date was in the bathroom.'

Colour stained Karl's cheeks. Embarrassment? Anger? Max didn't really care which, as long as Mr Oily left Cyn alone. The woman Karl'd been flirting with pretended to look out at the view from the balcony rail.

'I don't think this is any of your business—Mark, was it?'

'Max,' Max corrected coolly, not in the least fazed by the other man's puerile attempt to put him down. 'Actually, it is. Cyn keeps her private life that way—*private*. Which is fine, except sometimes it can lead to an embarrassing situation where people misunderstand.'

'Are you trying to say she's seeing *you*?' Karl asked.

Max folded his arms and leaned casually against the door. 'Put it this way, if she was seeing you, you'd know exactly what she was doing last weekend.' At Karl's surprised look, Max added softly, 'And I do.'

'I don't believe you.'

Max shrugged. 'That's your problem. But thank you for taking care of her for me. I'm here now, so you're free to carry on with whatever work you need to do.'

Before Karl could remonstrate further, Max strolled away. Very coolly. Very casually. And he was going to make damned sure he found Cyn before Fiennes did.

CHAPTER NINE

MAX scanned the room until he saw Cyn, then made his way over to her, making sure he stood between her and the balcony door.

'Hi, Cyn. How are you?'

Her eyes widened. Was she pleased to see him, annoyed, embarrassed? He wasn't sure. Her face was giving nothing away.

'Oh. Max. Hello.'

Her tone wasn't giving anything away, either. Cool and very, very polite.

He forced a smile to his face. 'So which is your favourite of the installations?'

'Installations?'

'The art,' he said softly. 'We're at the launch party for a new gallery, remember?'

'Yeah.' She rubbed a hand over her eyes. 'Sorry. It's been a heavy week.'

Max decided not to analyse that statement too deeply. He didn't want to know what 'heavy' meant, particularly if it had anything to do with that jerk on the balcony. The idea of Mr Oily keeping Cyn awake, causing her to make those soft little ohs of pleasure as he aroused her, discovering exactly where and how she liked being touched and kissed… Max found his hands balling into fists again.

'I've been troubleshooting for a major client,' she explained.

So she'd been working late—not spending every night making love. He relaxed for a second, then got indignant on her behalf again. If she'd been working stupid hours, there was even less excuse for that sleaze-bag to be messing her about! She needed cosseting, not being lied to. And Mr Oily wasn't the one to do it.

'How about you?'

'Hmm?' He'd completely missed her question, because he'd been staring at her mouth. Remembering. Hungering. Wanting to lean forward and take a tiny bite. 'Sorry.'

'Were you involved with—' she gestured towards the ceiling '—the building?'

He shook his head. 'I use mainly reclaimed materials—and I keep the original features as far as possible. They haven't, here.'

She didn't look any the wiser. Well, he knew how boring he could get on his favourite subject. His family tried bravely to listen to him, but their eyes always glazed over after a while. Maybe he should shut up. Now.

'So you're an art fan, then?' she asked.

'Me? Um…' Not this kind of art. 'I'm a little more… let's say…*traditional* in my outlook.'

She grinned. 'Dinosaur rock and prehistoric art, eh?'

He'd forgotten how her eyes crinkled at the corner when she smiled. And she had dimples. Very *cute* dimples. He only just stopped himself reaching out to touch.

'So is your client here yet?' she asked.

'No. And I think I'd rather get to see him somewhere quieter. Some place where we can talk about buildings without having to yell over the chatter of the crowd.' He smiled at her. 'Can I get you a drink?'

'Thanks, but I'm fine. Actually, I'm on my way home.'

'Home?' An image of Cyn lying on his sofa flashed into his mind and his knees went weak. God, he wanted to touch her. Taste her. Trail his mouth along her pulse points and feel the tell-tale beat speeding up.

She gave him a weary smile. 'I'm really only here because the gallery's my client and there's often a last-minute glitch or two that needs fixing. But everything's fine with the system, it's been a long week and I'm shattered. I just want to go home and curl up on the sofa with a good film.'

Curling up on the sofa sounded good. Curling up on the sofa with a good film and Cyn's body tucked in front of his sounded even better. Especially if she—

Uh. He needed to concentrate. 'How are you planning to get home?' If she was expecting Karl the Sleaze-bag to escort her, this might be a little tricky. But no way was he going to let Mr Oily take her home.

'Taxi. I've just ordered one.' She inched away from him. 'Well, it was nice to see you again.'

'Where are you going?'

She frowned. 'What is this, twenty questions? If you must know, I'm just going to tell Karl that my taxi's on its way.'

'Don't do that!' He grabbed her wrist. 'I mean… It's cold outside and you'll freeze in that dress. I'll go and tell him for you.'

She stared at him as if he'd grown two heads. 'But you don't know who Karl is.'

He didn't think she'd react too well if he told her he'd looked up Karl's profile on the company website and knew *exactly* who the man was. Or that he'd been childish enough to introduce himself to Karl and give his firmest handshake—before staking his territory and making sure

Fiennes knew that Cyn was off limits to anyone except Max. Then he had a lightbulb moment. 'He was the guy I saw you with earlier, right? Tall, blond?' And a louse.

'Yeah.'

'So I have a good memory. I can remember what he looks like. I'll find him for you.'

'Thank you, but I'll manage. Would you mind…?' She stared pointedly at his hand, which was still curled round her wrist.

He couldn't let her go. 'Cyn, sometimes men aren't what you think they are.'

'You can say that again,' she told him wryly.

Ouch. Well, maybe he'd deserved that. 'No, I mean…' He sighed. 'Look, you've got something going with the guy. I can see that. And I'm not trying to interfere…'

Completely untrue. He was interfering, big time. Because he didn't want her having something going with Mr Oily. She deserved better.

'I don't want to see you hurt.'

'Hurt? What are you talking about?'

'Just that maybe Karl isn't the right one for you.'

'Max, what are you…?' Her voice faded and she looked as stunned as he felt.

Did she sense it, too? The same warm, sweet feeling that was flowing through his veins? All he had to do was lean forward, so very slightly, and touch his mouth to hers. Just as he had last weekend. Just as he had when they'd danced together. And then all the noise, all the crowds around them would vanish. It would be just the two of them, their body heat rising, their bodies moulding—

Oh-h-h. He took a step back and dropped her wrist. This wasn't supposed to happen. He wasn't supposed to get this surge of desire running through him every time he touched her. He wasn't supposed to get hard every time he looked at her mouth. He was always in control—he didn't get swept away with his feelings.

Karl. Think about the sleaze-bag. She wanted to know why Max didn't want her to see him. 'I think he's busy. With a client,' he added, inspired. It was almost the truth; busy—yes, client—no. But it might head her off. He didn't want her to be with Fiennes, but he didn't want her to get hurt, either. 'Why don't we just leave a message for him at Reception?'

'We?'

'Yeah. I'll wait with you until your taxi comes.'

She shook her head. 'Thanks, but I really don't think it's necessary.'

'Look, you've had enough of the party. So have I. Shame we can't share a taxi.'

'Well, we don't live anywhere near each other.'

Yes. His office happened to be at his home, in Bayswater, and she lived in Islington. The opposite side of London. They definitely wouldn't go the same way home by taxi. But there was another way they could travel together.

'Why don't we take the tube? I can see you home, then carry on round on the Circle Line to mine.' It would mean a couple of extra changes of line for him, onto the Northern Line and then back to the Circle Line. So what?

'Max—'

The more he thought about it, the more he liked the idea. And he'd just had an even better one. 'I don't know about you, but I could do with some fresh air. Why don't we get our coats, take the tube to Bank station, and walk alongside the Thames?'

From the look on her face, he knew he'd said the wrong thing. He'd panicked. A few seconds ago he'd told her not to go out onto the balcony because she'd freeze. Now he was suggesting going for a walk by the river. A complete contradiction; don't go outside; yes, let's go outside. She must be thinking he was such an idiot.

Her words confirmed she knew he'd been trying to distract her. 'Max, what's happening on the balcony?'

'Nothing to worry about,' he said.

'Then why are you trying to stop me going out there?' she asked mildly.

He sighed. 'Look, I just don't want you getting hurt. You deserve better.'

She smiled. 'Karl's chatting someone up, isn't he?'

Max'd been about to say, 'Don't shoot the messenger'—but then he frowned. Her question suggested she knew exactly what Karl was like. And she was *smiling*. But shouldn't she be crying or wanting to pull the other woman's hair, or something? Just as he'd wanted to punch Karl when Mr Oily had taken Cyn on the balcony to kiss her? 'How did you know?'

She shrugged. 'Because Karl's a player. He dates a different girl every week.'

Umm. That sounded rather too much like Max himself for comfort. But that wasn't the point. 'And you still went out with him, knowing this?'

'I'm not going out with Karl. He doesn't do commitment.'

Max blinked. She'd just said the c-word. The word that could wreck everything between them before it had even started. And she'd just confirmed his worst fears. She wasn't going out with Karl because he didn't do commitment. Which meant… 'You're looking for commitment.'

Was she?

Cyn had always sworn she wouldn't make her mother's mistakes. She'd learned the hard way that men didn't commit—the number of 'uncles' in her past taught her that. They'd always been there for a while, then let her mum down. Right from the first one, who'd been a rebound from her father.

So Cyn hadn't expected commitment from her boyfriends. Maybe it was a self-fulfilling prophecy; because she'd always stayed that little bit detached, it had always been easy for her relationships to end. Neither she nor her boyfriends had wanted commitment.

Did she want commitment now? The more she thought about it, the more she was sure she didn't. Her mum was the one who had dreams of being married and settling down. Cyn wanted something else. She wanted to be a star in her world. A top-notch programmer and project manager, respected by all.

Which meant giving commitment to her job, not her social life.

Now she thought about it, all her crushes had been on unobtainable men. Film and rock stars as a teenager, men she knew she might see on stage but would never, ever, meet, so it was safe to fall in love with them. And she'd been really picky about dating, to the point where she even had a reputation of being unavailable.

Maybe Lisa was right and her grey suits *were* suits of armour. Anonymous business clothes that meant that men wouldn't be looking at her legs or down her cleavage, but would listen to her ideas and take her seriously in her job instead. She realised that Max was staring at her—and she hoped fervently that she hadn't said any of her thoughts aloud. 'Sorry, I didn't catch that.'

'I said, you're looking for commitment.'

She shrugged. 'I'm committed to my job.'

'So, you and Karl—it isn't serious?'

'He's a colleague, that's all. But he's a nice guy,' she

added, not wanting Max to think badly of Karl. So he might be chatting up another woman, mere minutes after Cyn had told him it wouldn't work between them—but that didn't make Karl a complete louse. 'He wanted to be sure I'd get home tonight.'

'I'm a nice guy, too.'

Mmm, and with the kind of smile that made her weak at the knees. Tonight, Max was wearing black trousers and a black round-necked cashmere sweater. All he needed was the earring and the bandanna, and he'd look like a pirate. Dark, dangerous and utterly gorgeous. And she really wasn't sure it was a good idea to leave the party with him.

'I'd like to be sure that you get home tonight. So let me go with you.' Another one of those killer smiles. How the hell was she supposed to resist that? 'And come for a walk, first.'

'You said it was freezing outside,' she reminded him.

'It's March. And it's not that cold—remember, the centre of London's always three or four degrees warmer than anywhere else in the country.'

Enlightenment dawned. 'You just didn't want me seeing Karl—' how could she put this? '—with someone else.'

He nodded. 'It's not pleasant, catching your partner being…' he paused, as if searching for a word, then looked rueful '…unfaithful.'

Had that happened to him? Was that why he threw himself into his work and didn't date? She wasn't sure whether she wanted to hug him, kiss him better—or kiss him until he forgot what day it was, let alone whatever had happened in his past.

Just in time, she bit the suggestion back and mumbled, 'Yeah.'

'You have a coat, don't you?' he asked.

She nodded. 'A wrap.'

'Then let's go.'

Five minutes later, she'd cancelled her taxi, left a message for Karl that a friend was seeing her home and she'd call him at work on Monday, and Max was sliding her wrap around her shoulders. His fingers touched her bare skin, very briefly, and desire shimmered down her spine. Her body could still remember the touch of his: the way he'd danced with her, the way he'd kissed her... The way he'd stroked her until she was almost hyperventilating...

She wasn't far off that now.

'You okay?' he asked.

'Yeah,' she lied. 'Just cold.'

'Here.' He began stripping off his long black coat.

'No, no. I'll be fine in a second.' She'd forgotten his Sir Galahad tendencies. Stupid. He'd rescued her at the wedding and he'd rescued her again tonight. He probably thought she'd been hinting.

She hadn't.

But the idea of wearing his coat—still warm from his body, sheathed in his scent—sent another shiver of longing through her.

'You're really cold.'

'No, no. It's a nice night. Very mild, for March.'

Great. And now she was talking about the weather. How cheesy could she get?

He gave her a sidelong look, as if he didn't quite believe she wasn't really cold, but then nodded. 'Sure you're up to a walk?'

What did he think she was—a woman like one of those professional invalids during Victorian times who only managed to nibble on a corner of a sandwich and then had to go to bed for a week to recover? 'Sure. Where are we going?'

'Depends which station the first train goes to—either Tower Gateway, so we can walk along Tower Bridge and then along the river, or Bank, and we'll come out at the Monument.'

'Sounds good.'

The first train took them to Bank. As they walked through the low-ceilinged tunnel towards the Monument exit, they heard a busker tuning his guitar, then launching into the opening of a song. She glanced at Max, discovered that he was looking at her, and smiled. 'I love this one.'

'Me too.' His eyes crinkled at the corners. Such sexy eyes. She nearly stumbled as a wave of longing hit her. She wanted to see those eyes heat up as he undressed her…

'It's good to hear some decent music. I really hated the faux-jazz they were playing tonight,' he said.

'It wasn't *that* bad.'

'Yes, it was. Not up to the standard of—' Max named a sultry female vocalist.

'I thought you hated slushy ballads?'

'I like jazz. Piano, that is.' He grinned again. 'But I like smoky voices too.' His expression grew more intense as his eyes raked over her face and settled on her lips.

Cyn's pulse-rate eased up a notch at the thought of Max kissing her. Of him pausing to kiss her under every single lamppost on the Embankment.

She sucked in a breath, telling herself to take it easy. It was just a walk.

A walk with *possibilities*.

And the possibilities sent ripples of excitement down her spine.

CHAPTER TEN

'I NEVER really get to see this part of London,' Cyn said. 'Unless I have a client meeting in the middle of the City, but even then I don't see much more than the area between the tube station and the client's office.'

'It's beautiful. Look up,' Max said.

She did, and blinked in surprise. 'Wow. I didn't realise the buildings were so tall—or so pretty.'

'You wouldn't, if you're hurrying to an office or to catch a train. Most people just see what's at eye level, or possibly look at their feet. This is the London nobody ever sees. It's a shame the Monument's closed at night—there's an amazing view from the top. But come and look at this.' He shepherded her over to London Bridge.

The sky was overcast so the Thames looked dark; she could see ripples on the water, blown by the wind. Down-river, Tower Bridge was lit up, a streak of red running along its span; globe-like lanterns lit the path along the Thames.

'London by night,' he said softly. 'It's beautiful. Let's have a closer look at the lamps.'

'The lamps?' Mystified, Cyn followed Max down some steps to the Thames pathway.

'The Sturgeon Lamp-standards, created by George

Vulliamy,' he said. 'They're cast iron—every one has a sea creature wrapped round it, and either the date it was made or Queen Victoria's initials at the base. The further east you walk, the newer the lamppost; they were made specially to illuminate the Albert Embankment.'

'I never knew that,' Cyn said.

'Tell you something else I bet you never knew. You know the lion on Westminster Bridge?'

'Mmm-hmm.'

'It used to be painted bright red, because it used to stand on the roof of the Red Lion Brewery. But the factory was damaged in the war and it was knocked down to build the Royal Festival Hall for the Festival of Britain in nineteen fifty-one. That was when King George VI had the lion moved to Waterloo station, and finally to Westminster Bridge. The lion was one of the last products made from Coade stone—and it weighs thirteen tons.'

Cyn gave him a sidelong look. 'I bet you've got all the volumes of Pevsner.' The architectural history of Britain. And she'd bet he read and digested them, too; they wouldn't be on his bookshelves just for show. She could imagine him sitting curled up on the sofa, studying the book; he'd wear that intense look…focused—just as he did when he was making love…

She pushed the thought away. They were just going for a walk, that was all. She was *not* going to leap on him. Even though she wanted to.

'I've got all the Pevsners for London and elsewhere,' he admitted. 'They're fascinating. Every time I dip into them, I find something new.'

'And then you go and see for yourself?'

He nodded. 'I know. It's sad.'

'No. You just really love your job. You do what you love, and you love what you do.' She knew what she'd love him to do, right now. Take her into his arms, hold her very, very close—so close that her body was almost merged with his—and kiss her. Take tiny nibbles at her bottom lip, teasing and coaxing and demanding until she opened her mouth to let him kiss her properly. Slide his mouth down her neck, rediscovering all the sensitive areas that made her gasp when he touched her. And—

Oh, for goodness' sake. Anyone would think she was a giddy teenager, not a sensible twenty-seven-year-old. She just hoped she didn't have a stupid look on her face. Or, if she did, that he'd guess what had put it there.

Do what you love, and love what you do. Cyn was the first person he could ever remember understanding the passion he had for his job. Max smiled at her. 'Most people start snoring when I talk about work. Thanks for staying awake.'

'Actually, it's interesting. And I'd rather see something like this with someone who knows exactly what they're looking at and can point things out to me.' She smiled back. 'Were you always interested in architecture?'

'Pretty much.' Maybe she was just being polite; maybe not. He gave into the impulse to tell her. 'There was this old tumbledown manor house in the village where I lived as a child. All the kids used to sneak in through a hole in the fence and play there. The other kids were all more interested in making dens in the garden, but I found a window I could climb through. I used to wander round the house and imagine what it looked like years before, when the windows weren't broken and the paint wasn't peeling off and there were carpets instead of crumbling floorboards.'

She frowned. 'If it was in that sort of state, it sounds dangerous. You could have been hurt.'

He nodded. 'Our parents didn't know what we were up to. Well, not until I got caught there, a few weeks after the house was sold. The other kids stayed away, but I couldn't—I wanted to see what they were doing to the house, so I sneaked back through the fence. The builders caught me trespassing and marched me off to my parents.'

'Ouch.'

Ouch didn't even begin to describe it. He could still remember his mother shouting at him. At the time, he'd thought it unfair. Now he was older, he had a different perspective and could recognise the panic in her voice. 'My mum went mad. She said I could have been really badly hurt.' He spread his hands. 'I was only ten. I didn't think about things like broken glass and severed arteries, or bricks landing on my head from a great height, or falling through the floor and getting stuck and people having to send a search party out to find me. I just wanted to see how they were making the house better.'

'And did you?'

He nodded. 'When I explained what I'd been doing there—that I hadn't been smashing windows or vandalising the old place—Mick, the foreman on the building site, lent me a hard hat and gave me a proper tour. He showed me the architect's plans and how to read them, and I was hooked. I spent every spare minute there, watching them restore the house little by little.'

'Did you skip school?'

He chuckled. 'I would have done, if I'd thought I could get away with it. But Mick said that maths was important—if I was serious about a career in restoration, I'd need to know about angles and calculations, load-bearing walls and the like. Science was important, too, because I'd learn about the properties of different materials. And history was really important because you can't do a proper restoration job if you don't have a feel for the history of the place.' He smiled. 'Then, in the last term of middle school, we had to do a project on a building in the village. Everyone else did theirs on the church—but I did mine on the old house.'

'An excuse to help with the restoration?' she guessed.

He nodded. 'I wrote down everything that was happening, drew bits of the building before it was restored and then everything afterwards. I'd never been interested in art before, but that's when I discovered that I could draw. Not portraits—I don't sketch people.' Not usually. Though he'd found himself sketching Cyn, the other day. Doodling while he was on the phone. 'Though I sketched all the craftsmen at work and explained what they were doing— how they replaced all the worm-eaten woodwork, matched the carvings in the mantelpieces, and made new mouldings and cornices for the ceilings.'

'Were they okay about you sketching them while they were at work?'

He smiled. 'Oh, yes. They loved the fact that someone young was actually interested in the old techniques instead of wanting to do things with a fast turnover and a quick profit, so they talked me through exactly what they were doing. Then I pleaded my case with Mick and got him to give me a job in the school holidays—not a proper paid job, but I wanted an excuse to hang around the house without getting in the way. I drove my parents insane until they agreed. I just did a bit of fetching and carrying, at first, taking them mugs of tea and stuff, but his team realised it wasn't just a fad with me. So they taught me the basics, and let me practise making joints or carving decorations on offcuts of wood. I could even show you the precise bit of wall that I plastered.' He grinned. 'They probably redid it after I'd gone home, but as far as I'm concerned that was *my* bit of wall.'

Cyn was laughing, but he was pretty sure she was laughing with him, not at him.

'Your parents must have been really proud of you,' she said. 'Ten or eleven years old, and you'd already sorted out your career *and* got a job—you knew exactly what you wanted to do.'

Proud of him? Hmm. That was a sticking point. 'The thing is, my dad's a doctor. I was supposed to follow in his footsteps—except I wanted to make buildings better, not people.'

She took his hand, very briefly, and squeezed it. 'I'm sure he understood. You were following your dreams.'

Max wasn't so sure. He could still see the disappointment in his father's eyes when he'd realised that Max wasn't going to change his mind, do science A levels and then study medicine. Max had chosen maths, technical drawing, English and history, followed by a degree in architecture. He'd left it to his younger brother to go into the family business.

'I sometimes feel that I let my family down,' Max said softly. 'Every choice I made, it wasn't what they expected of me. What they'd hoped I'd do. Studying architecture instead of medicine. Going to London instead of settling down. Taking the risk of going it alone instead of staying with a steady, long-established architectural practice.' Even thinking about it made his skin itch with guilt, and he wanted to get away from the subject. Fast. 'What about you? Did you always want to do computer programming?'

'I was good at maths,' she said. 'I liked numbers—the fact they're so ordered and they behave in a logical pattern. You know where you are with numbers.'

Whereas you were never completely sure where you were with people. Yeah, he could understand that.

'But it meant I always finished my work early. And I got bored, waiting for the others to catch up, so I used to read a book under the table. When I was on my third detention in a row for reading in class, the headmaster sent for me. I thought I was going to be in trouble, but he was really nice about it. His specialist subject was maths; he'd looked at my work and thought I was probably bored in class.'

'Which you were.'

She nodded. 'The school was pretty flexible about time-tabling, so I switched to the maths class of a higher year group and took the exams a couple of years early.' She smiled. 'Then the headmaster introduced me to computer programming. I loved it—I loved the way you could feed in a set of figures and make something *happen*. I remember the first time I wrote a program that printed out a huge letter "C", all made up of just one letter. The rest of the class just couldn't get the hang of it and spent ages rehashing their code—it took them weeks to print out their own initial letter—but to me it was all so obvious. All you had to do was be logical and work through the program in an ordered way.'

Logic and order. Welcome to Cyn's world. 'So you made up your own programs at home?'

'Only in theory, because Mum couldn't afford to buy me a computer. I made excuses, but eventually the headmaster guessed it was because of my family circumstances.' From the look on her face, that still rankled. 'He came up with a couple of suggestions, but no way was I going to accept charity. So I stopped doing the extra lessons at lunchtime.'

Proud and determined to go it alone. He liked that. 'So you just left it there?'

She wrinkled her nose. 'I would have done, but then the headmaster suggested I talked to the local computer dealer and ask them for a Saturday job.'

'So you could learn about programming there?'

She shook her head. 'Not at first—I just did the filing, worked the cash till and made coffee for the technicians. But I was reading everything I could get my hands on, including borrowing books about programming from one of the technicians, and I begged my boss for some time on the computer in my breaks. He realised I was serious about it, so he let me help Philip, the senior technician, build a system from scratch. Mum wouldn't take any housekeeping from me, so I saved my wages and spent them on second-hand components, then built my first system at home. With a bit of help from Philip, that is.'

Max had never had to worry about money. He'd taken the family computer for granted. Cyn's background was so very, very different—but she understood him. Understood the need to know more and more and more. Understood the need to be the best at what he did. Because, deep down, she was just the same.

'What sort of programs did you write?'

'Computer games.'

'What kind of games?'

She smiled. 'Nothing with huge graphics needing lots of memory—not with the kind of machines we used back then! They were just card games and word games, with a little bit of animation to make it more fun. It helped my friends relax when they'd been revising for exams.'

And it got her the all-important acceptance among her peers. Though probably not from Michelle Wilson and her cronies: they'd have used it as yet another point of difference to underline. The fact that Cyn understood numbers.

Then he frowned. 'That game Lisa's always playing at lunchtime…is that one of yours?'

'The wordbug one, where you make words out of other words?'

'Yeah. She and her mates send each other emails comparing their high scores.'

Cyn chuckled. 'That's *years* old.'

'Haven't you thought about selling it? Setting up on your own?'

She shook her head. 'No, it's too much hassle, what with the copyright and the distribution—even though I know I could probably distribute it on the web. No, it's not what I want. I wrote that for fun. Besides, it's too old-fashioned to be a fast-seller, so no company would take it on; most people nowadays prefer the shoot-'em-up arcade games with plenty of graphics.' She shrugged. 'Anyway, I like working at RCS. I get to play with different systems and talk to different clients—they tell me what they want, and I make it happen. I love seeing their faces when they realise I've built exactly what they needed, and kept it simple so they won't have to spend months retraining their staff. Plus I love Gus, Mark and Rob.'

'Gus, Mark and Rob?' he queried, his hackles rising. Who the hell were they?

'My team.'

Well, of course her team would be male. Most techies were male. That little stab of jealousy was ridiculous. Grow *up*, he told himself.

Maybe she'd realised what lay behind his silence, because she added, 'They're like the kid brothers I never had.'

There was a hint of wistfulness in her voice. Though, if she'd been an only child *and* had gone to a school where she hadn't really fitted in, she was bound to have been lonely as a kid.

Max suddenly realised that they were standing by Tower Bridge. 'Um. Sorry, I didn't mean to drag you out for this long.' He'd just lost track of time with Cyn, telling her about his beloved buildings and learning what made her tick. They'd just wandered along the river bank—and he hadn't been aware of anything else except the woman by his side. 'Sorry. It was only meant to be a bit of fresh air, something to blow the cobwebs out.'

'I've enjoyed it.'

'Me, too.' And he didn't want it to stop. 'We can get the tube from here and change at Moorgate—though we'd probably have to wait for ages for a train.' Not that he'd mind waiting with her. 'Or we could walk back to Bank again.' It was a long way, but please let her want to walk back again. Let her want to spend time talking to him.

'We could see if the busker's still there,' she said.

His smile felt a mile wide. 'So walking's okay with you?'

'Yeah, it's fine.'

Walking it was, then. Max resisted the urge to punch the air and cheer.

And talk about a back-to-front courtship. Last week, they'd spent the night together. Skin to skin, wrapped in each other's arms. They'd made love on Sunday morning—as far as they could go without a condom, that was. Tonight, this was more like their first date. Getting to know each other, walking hand in hand. He'd told her things he hadn't even told Gina, mainly because Gina had always seen his work as a rival and had never wanted to talk about it. Cyn would never see architecture and restoration as the 'other woman', because she felt the same way about her own job. Her job was who she was; just as his job defined who *he* was.

They turned round and started to retrace their steps. 'You never know, the busker might do a request for us,' Max said.

Cyn laughed. 'He might.'

Mmm. Max thought he could ask for a song that reflected the way he was feeling right now—the way he wanted to kiss Cyn. Remind himself of how she tasted. Remind her of the way things sizzled between them when they were skin to skin.

The sky was overcast, though every one of Vulliamy's globe lanterns looked like a full moon reflected in one of those infinity mirrors, if they stood between two of them and looked from side to side, seeing the lights stretch on and on and on.

It was all the excuse he needed. Max stopped beneath one of the lamps, spun Cyn to face him, and yanked her into his arms.

CHAPTER ELEVEN

CYN was hallucinating. Definitely. In real life, she was stuck in the middle of the party, talking to the client, pretending to smile and have a fabulous time when inwardly she was desperate to get a taxi, go home and fall into bed. No way was she standing under a lamp on the bank of the Thames on an overcast evening in early March, with Max's arms round her. No way was his hand inside her wrap and sliding down her spine, pressing her tightly against his body. No way were his lips brushing lightly against hers, tiny butterfly kisses that aroused her so much she was completely unable to keep a cool head. She wasn't really here, tipping her head back and offering him her mouth…was she?

She opened her eyes. Max's eyes were only centimetres from her own. So close that she could see his unfairly long black lashes and the dark navy rim around his slate-blue irises. His pupils were huge with desire, and he had that intense look on his face that she remembered from earlier tonight and the previous weekend. The same look that he'd given her just before he'd kissed his way down her body and sent her spiralling over the edge.

"'If ever any beauty I did see,'" Max whispered, "'Which I desired, and got, 'twas but a dream of thee.'"

His voice was low, husky with longing. But she didn't quite understand. Was he saying he thought she was beautiful? She must be hearing things. Cyn knew she was nothing out of the ordinary. She was a little under average height, and if she was honest with herself she could do with toning up and losing about twenty pounds...

And then she forgot to think when Max kissed her again. All she could do was slide her hands into his silky dark hair and kiss him back. The rest of the world didn't exist any more. Just Max, the warmth of his mouth against hers and the hardness of his body crushed against her. Just Max, and his hand sliding up over her belly to cup one breast.

She forgot where they were. All she wanted was for him to rip down the last barriers between them: the lace of her bra and the silky-soft material of her dress were way too much. She needed to feel his hands against her skin. Properly. Feel his thumb rubbing against her nipple.

And she hardly dared think about what she wanted his mouth to do to her.

As if he could read her mind, he eased his hand under the neckline of her dress. The tips of his fingers reached the edge of her bra, and Cyn began to quiver. He was still kissing her, his mouth demanding more and more, and then, at last, his hand cupped her breast properly. Skin to skin.

She shuddered as his thumb rubbed against her nipple. The friction was good, but it still wasn't enough. She wanted more. Needed more. She rocked her hips against him; he broke the kiss and took a sharp intake of breath.

'Do you have any idea what you do to me?' he asked, his voice husky.

'The same as you do to me,' she answered in a whisper.

'I want you.'

'Yes.'

She wasn't sure what she was saying yes to. Yes, she knew he wanted her? Yes, she wanted him, too? Yes, there were only the two of them right here and now, so what was there to stop them?

His hand was inside her dress now. And if there were any passers-by, they'd have no idea, because his long coat and her wrap hid everything. They'd just think that she and Max were sharing a passionate kiss.

Friday-night lovers.

It wasn't as if she'd drunk too much champagne. Knowing that she was already so tired more than one glass of wine would send her straight to sleep, she'd stuck to sparkling mineral water at the party. No, it wasn't alcohol making her feel this reckless. It was Max. The fact that she could feel how hard he was, through his trousers. He wanted her as much as she wanted him—she'd turned him on that much.

The memory of what they'd done last weekend was too much for her. She wanted him to make love with her again. Here and now. Her surroundings just faded away; all she was aware of was Max. The muskiness of his scent; the taste of his mouth on hers; the feel of his fingertips on her skin.

She slid her fingers underneath the hem of his sweater. Soft, soft cashmere. And even softer skin underneath. His belly was washboard-flat—though she didn't think that Max was like Karl, heading for the gym every night after work.

He broke the kiss again and his breath hissed. 'Cyn, if you keep touching me like this, I'm not going to be responsible for—'

The rest of his words were choked off as she whispered, 'Good,' and undid the button of his trousers.

The lamplight hid nothing: she could see shock sliding over his face, swiftly replaced with a surge of need.

'Yes,' he ground out, pressing her backwards until her back was braced against the lamppost.

Knowing that what she was doing was hidden by their clothes, she slid the zipper downwards. Slowly. Very slowly.

He whimpered, and she took pity on him. 'Is this what you want?' she asked, sliding her fingers under the hem of his jockey shorts and curling them round his shaft.

'Oh-h-h. Yes.' His voice sounded cracked, as if he'd had to force the words out, and his fingers tightened on her breast. 'Cyn. I need…need to touch you, too. Properly.'

The longing in his voice made her feel even more reckless. 'Then what's stopping you?' she asked, her voice soft and almost taunting. 'Who's going to see?' Nobody. Not with her wrap and his coat hiding them.

He kissed her again. Hard. And then she felt him bunch the skirt of her dress at her waist, pulling the hem upwards until it was high enough to give him the access he wanted. His hand slid between her thighs, and she felt him shiver as he realised she was wearing hold-up stockings.

He nuzzled the skin below her ear. 'If I'd known you were wearing stockings… Did you wear them for *him*?'

Was that jealousy? Oh, bless. There was no need. 'I wore them for me,' she said softly. 'But you like them?'

'Oh, yeah.' His voice dropped in pitch. 'I like them. I like that I can touch you.'

His fingers drifted over the warm, soft skin of her inner thigh, teasing her. And then it was her turn to shiver as he cupped her sex. She could feel the warmth of his hand, feel the blood pulsing in his fingertips—as hard and fast as her own blood was pumping round her body.

Only a thin barrier of cotton and lace separated them, but it was still too much of an obstruction. 'Touch me,' she invited huskily.

He didn't need her to ask twice. His fingers quested, found the lacy edge of her knickers, and pulled it aside.

She tilted her hips and widened her stance slightly as he eased one finger into her.

'So warm and wet and ready for me,' he murmured against her mouth. 'I want you so much.'

Mmm, she could feel that!

'I need you inside me,' she said, stroking him. 'Now.'

'Yes,' he breathed and jammed his mouth over hers.

Just as he started to lift her higher against the lamppost, ready to enter her, a loud wolf-whistle split the air.

They both froze.

Their surroundings suddenly rushed back in on her. They were practically at the point of having sex on the middle of the Embankment. In full public view. They could both get arrested for this!

'Stay exactly where you are,' Max muttered to Cyn, 'or I think we're both going to get very, very embarrassed.' He kept his body shielding her, turning only his head to face the passer-by who'd whistled at them. 'Ish Friday night,' he slurred. 'Kish my woman under the moon. Thash amorray, right?' He broke into the opening lines of 'That's Amore', waving one hand at the globe lamppost as he warbled.

'Better get home to bed, mate,' the passer-by said, laughing.

'Yesh. Bed,' Max said, laughing back. 'Thash the righ' idea. Thash amorray!'

He held Cyn tightly. 'Stay put,' Max warned her quietly. 'As long as he thinks we're drunk and happy and we're not going to be any trouble, we're going to get away with this.'

The man whistled again; when he'd moved on, Max swiftly restored order to Cyn's clothes, and then to his own.

'I can't believe we just…' Cyn choked. Her skin felt tight with embarrassment. They'd been caught in the most compromising of situations. With her dress hiked up, his trousers undone, and their hands where they definitely shouldn't have been in public!

'Lucky he said something when he did. Five seconds more, and all hell would have broken loose around us and I wouldn't have heard or known or cared,' Max said. He bent to whisper in her ear. 'Because I'd have been inside you. Where I still want to be, right now.'

Oh, Lord. It was where she wanted him to be, too.

He kissed the tip of her nose. 'I'm sorry. I...' His gaze held hers. Challenging. 'I just wanted to kiss you. And I got carried away. *Very* carried away.'

She wasn't complaining. She'd wanted him to kiss her, too. And more. And she'd got just as carried away. She'd been the one to start undoing clothes, after all.

He looked as dazed as she felt. 'I don't normally do things like this,' he said.

Like what? Almost having sex in public? 'Me, neither. But I was going to ring you,' she admitted.

'Ring me?'

'Mmm. And ask you—' She stopped dead and colour scorched into her cheeks. If she told him what she'd wanted, she'd sound *desperate*. She needed to sort out the right words in her head, first.

He took her hand, drew it up to his lips and kissed each fingertip in turn. 'Ask me what?'

Oh, Lord. She couldn't think when he did that. When he sucked the tip of her middle finger and held her gaze, as if telling her where else he wanted to suck. Her nipples were so hard that they hurt, and there was a pulse beating rapidly between her thighs. Where he'd been touching her only seconds ago.

She wanted him. Now.

'I want you to...' To have an affair with me. An all-guns-blazing, mad, passionate affair. Just so we can get this thing out of our systems and go back to normal.

But her mouth wasn't working in sync with her mind. 'I don't do this sort of thing,' she blurted out. 'This isn't me.'

'Just you and your job. I know,' he said. 'I'm usually focused on mine, too—but I haven't stopped thinking about you all week.'

And if she'd had time to think about anything else other than work, this week—if she hadn't just put the hours in until her mind was too numb to do anything than shut down the second she fell into bed—she wouldn't have stopped thinking about him, either.

He was still holding her hand; he rubbed his thumb against her palm. 'Those chocolates you sent me... I had all sorts of fantasies. About you. Eating chocolate off your skin,' he said.

Every single one of her nerve-endings was aware of Max. And every single one of them reacted to the picture he'd just conjured up: herself, naked, and Max drizzling warm melted chocolate onto her skin, then licking it off until she was quivering with need. Until she begged him to enter her, fill her body and ease away the ache his mouth had created.

'We're two of a kind,' Max said. 'Driven.'

Yeah. She could buy that.

He traced the outline of her face with his forefinger. 'I found myself sketching you, this week. On top of a blueprint I was working on. When I thought I was doodling on a piece of scrap paper during a phone call.' His breath hitched. 'And I never, ever get distracted from my work.'

'Neither do I. Until you.'

'But you were at the party with Karl tonight.'

'It was work.' As far as she was concerned, anyway. 'Not a *date* date,' Cyn said. She bit her lip. 'What are we going to do about this?'

'We've got a choice. Pretend it isn't happening and try and make sure we never cross each other's paths again…or see where it takes us.'

See where it took them. Spontaneous. Cyn didn't do spontaneous. She planned *everything*. Logic, order: she was safe with that. She knew where she was. Seeing where things took them… That was dangerous. It was like stepping onto marshy ground and hoping that luck would keep her to a solid path.

And she knew there was no such thing as luck. Just careful planning and hard work.

He cupped her face. 'We just have to trust each other.'

'I don't want to get hurt.' Her words blurted out from nowhere. But she knew where they'd come from: all the years she'd lain awake, hearing her mother crying over yet another man who'd let her down. Late at night, when Stacey had thought her daughter was asleep and wouldn't know, but Cyn had known. Every single time. And her heart had ached for Stacey, the woman who wanted to be loved but had never found the right one for her.

So Cyn hadn't even tried looking for The One. Because she knew he didn't exist.

'I don't want to get hurt, either,' Max said quietly. His eyes looked tortured. 'I can't promise you anything, Cyn. I can't promise commitment. I don't know if I have it in me. I've been there…and I messed it up. Big time.'

'You're divorced?'

'No. But I was serious about someone. Serious enough to be engaged.' He looked away. 'I still feel bad about what happened, but it just wouldn't have worked. I was too young. Gina and I didn't want the same things—she wanted marriage, a country cottage, four kids and a menagerie, and I just wasn't ready to settle down.'

She remembered his earlier comment about people

being unfaithful. 'What did you do—leave her for someone else?'

He shook his head. 'I couldn't be *that* much of a scumbag.'

'She left you for someone else?'

'No, I left her. But not for anyone else. It was for my job.' He sighed. 'We met at college. She was training to be a primary-school teacher. She was quiet and sweet and a little bit shy. I thought she was what I wanted. But I also thought we still had plenty of time, that we'd get our careers off the ground before we got married and started a family. She didn't see it that way. Her biological clock was ticking, and mine wasn't.'

'That's why you left her?'

Max nodded. 'Gina hated that I spent so much time at work. She didn't understand how I feel about my job, or that sometimes projects go haywire and I have to spend time fixing them.'

It was the same with her job. Building architecture, systems architecture… They had a lot in common.

'We rowed about it all the time. She was sure it'd be all right once we were married, but as the weeks went by I knew it wouldn't. She saw my job as a rival. And eventually I would have had to choose between them. If I chose her, I'd have to give up the only job I ever wanted to do. If I chose my job, I'd lose her. But we'd lost the magic anyway. It had got to the point where I saw her name on the screen of my mobile phone and I'd pretend I was in a meeting and ignore the call.' He grimaced. 'Which wasn't fair to either of us. So I called it off.'

'How far had you got with the wedding plans?'

'Pretty far,' he admitted. 'She'd bought her dress and ordered the flowers. She'd booked the horse and carriage. We'd even sent the invitations out.' He swallowed hard. 'I didn't behave well. I should never have let it go that far. We should never even have got engaged. But I...I suppose I wanted to make everyone happy.' He rubbed a hand across his eyes. 'I tried to be the man everyone wanted me to be—a devoted husband for Gina, a son who was settled for my parents. Except it wasn't me. When it came down to it, I couldn't do it. Because it just wasn't who I was. And I couldn't spend my life living someone else's dreams. Not at the expense of my own. I needed someone to share my dreams with me. Someone who had the same dreams.'

'So you did the right thing before it was too late,' Cyn said. 'You could have gone ahead with the wedding and ended up another statistic. If you hadn't given up your job, she'd have been unhappy; and if you *had* given it up, you'd have been unhappy. You would have ended up hating each other and forgetting about the good times.'

'That's what *I* said. But nobody else saw it that way. Everyone was so disappointed in me. They just saw me being selfish and racketing off to the bright lights of London.' He shook his head. 'It wasn't that at all. It wasn't the lights that drew me.'

'It was the buildings. The chance to make a difference. To bring them back to life,' she said softly.

'Yeah.' His eyes were haunted. 'I know now I definitely did the right thing for both of us—Gina's happily married now, with her second baby on the way. But I still hurt her at the time. I hurt her badly, because I couldn't commit. And I've kept all my relationships very light ever since. Nothing serious.'

He was warning her. Giving her the chance to back off now. He'd tried commitment before, to someone who was very like Cyn—someone who was quiet and shy. And it had gone badly wrong. On the other hand, Gina had seen herself in competition with Max's job, whereas Cyn understood—because she felt the same way about her own job. Had the same dream: to be the best in her field.

He'd been honest with her. And it sounded as if he was as much in the dark as she was about where they were going. 'Are you saying that maybe we should just walk away?' she asked.

'Too late,' he said softly. 'Because I think that's already going to hurt too much. There's something about you— something I can't even begin to explain to myself, so I don't have a chance in hell of explaining it to you. It's just…' He bent his head and brushed his lips lightly against hers. 'Come on. Let's walk to the station.'

He didn't let her hand go. And although in some respects it scared the hell out of her, in others it felt good just to walk with him in silence. No pressure of conversation; just the two of them, hand in hand.

Would they become lovers tonight? Would they carry on where they'd left off on the Embankment? Her pulse speeded up. Would they take the risk and trust each other?

CHAPTER TWELVE

BY THE time they reached the tube station, Max felt tense enough to grip marble with his bare hands and turn it to sand, though his fingers were laced very gently through Cyn's. Because he couldn't let her go tonight. He wanted her too much. Needed her.

God, her mouth was lush. Maybe one taste would clear his head. Just one.

Unable to help himself, he led her to a quieter, less brightly lit corner of the station, dragged her back into his arms, cradled the nape of her neck in one hand, and kissed her. Hard.

His other hand slid under her wrap. It was a shapeless piece of wool. So how come it turned him on so much? Probably because it made him think of *un*wrapping her, he acknowledged wryly. And the wrap was soft and warm, like her skin.

His hand drifted over the curve of her hip, then over her buttocks. He adored her curves.

He broke the kiss to nuzzle her cheek. 'I want you, Cyn,' he whispered. 'This is driving me crazy. I want to touch you. I want to taste you all over. I want to make love with you until neither of us can see straight—and then do it all over again.' And again. He had a feeling he could easily become greedy, where Cynthia Reynolds was concerned. Insatiable. 'There's nothing I want more than to take you to bed, right now. I want to carry you up the stairs to my bed. I want to strip every inch of clothing from you and explore you until we're both balancing right on the edge. And we'll fall together.' He brushed his mouth over hers again. 'Come home with me.'

'Max, I…I don't do this sort of thing. I'm not a player.'

'I know. But this thing between us…it's not going to go away.' He didn't know why. He just had this feeling that she might be The One. The one he'd been looking for without even realising it. Though if he told her that he might scare her off for good. Hell, he was scaring *himself* even by thinking it!

So he fell back on honesty. 'I don't know what's happening, either. It's crazy. Scary, even. All I know is I don't want to say goodnight to you. I don't want to take you home and leave you on your doorstep. I want to be with you,' he said, nuzzling her cheek. 'And you make me feel things I didn't think I'd ever feel. Tonight, I wanted to punch Karl Fiennes on the nose, beat my chest, haul you over my shoulder and carry you back to my cave.'

'And you'd have ended up with a hernia, sore knuckles and an assault charge,' she said dryly.

'The knuckles and police record would've been worth it. And I disagree about the hernia. You're not that heavy.' Just to prove it to her, he slid both hands under her buttocks, lifted her and pressed her back against the wall.

Oh-h-h. Bad move. Too close to how they'd been on the Embankment. If they were both naked—or at least in the same state of semi-undress they'd been under the lamp-post—all he'd have to do now was lower her, just a little. Tilt his hips, just a little. The tip of his penis would just nudge her entrance. And then his body would slide into hers. She'd be wrapped round him, warm and wet and...

He couldn't help a do-me-now-or-I'm-going-to-pass-out groan. And he couldn't help tilting his hips, pressing against her. Through their clothes, he knew she'd feel how hard he was. How much he wanted her.

Her eyes were dark and deep, and he could drown in them.

'Max. We're in a public place,' she reminded him, sounding slightly shocked.

'I know. And we shouldn't be doing this.' He let her slide down his body. 'Want to know something *really* bad?'

She quivered against him.

'If it hadn't been for that passer-by...'

'I know. We'd have had sex. In public.' Her voice sounded slightly husky.

'Worse than that, honey. It would've been *unprotected* sex in public.' And, even worse than that, he wasn't exactly shocked by the thought. Because he wanted Cyn with no barriers. He wanted her so badly, it hurt. And he couldn't remember ever feeling like this before.

Did The One exist?

And was Cyn that woman?

'Come home with me,' he said again. 'Let tomorrow take care of itself. Tonight it's just you and me.'

'Unprotected sex.'

She was shaking. With fear? 'No, of course not. I'll take care of you.' He punctuated his words with kisses. 'There's nothing to worry about.'

She said nothing, but her eyes were glittering. Unshed tears? Ah, hell. He stroked her cheek. 'I'm not going to hurt you, Cyn.'

'I'm not a player,' she said again. 'I don't do this sort

of thing. I don't have *time* for relationships.' She swallowed. 'I don't do one-night stands, either.'

'Technically, it isn't one.' He brushed the tip of his nose against hers. 'Remember last Sunday morning?'

'Yes.'

The word sounded like a sigh, a hiss of pleasure.

'That was the start. This is going to be more. Everything we couldn't do then—and then some.' He nibbled her lower lip. 'Come home with me, Cyn.' He held her close. 'Stay with me tonight.' His mouth brushed the sensitive spot by her ear. 'Make love with me, honey. Let's show each other how good it can be.'

'Yes.'

It took a few seconds to sink in. And then he went into meltdown.

She was going home with him.

He had no idea how they got through the ticket barrier. How they even got to the right platform. Because all he could think about was this amazing woman in his arms—and what was going to happen the second they walked through his front door.

When they got on the train, he pulled her onto his lap so she was cradled sideways in his arms. He wanted her close. He wanted to feel the warmth of her body against his. And besides, if he let her sit next to him, he had a feeling she'd go logical and sensible on him again. He didn't want to take the risk. He wanted her with him, all the way. He wanted her to feel just as hot and bothered as he did.

'Max,' she protested as he wrapped his arms round her waist and drew her even closer. 'There are loads of empty seats.'

'Mmm-hmm. I can see that.' He tightened his arms round her. 'But this is comfortable.' Well, it was for him.

'Put your arms round my neck and you won't feel so off balance.'

She wriggled on his lap, clearly embarrassed. 'I'm too heavy.'

'No, you're not.' Was she really worried about the fact she wasn't a stick insect? Well, he could do something about that. 'There's something I ought to tell you.'

He felt her tense, and smiled. 'Cyn. You know I'm an architect.'

'Yes.'

'So I appreciate form.'

'Ye-es.' She sounded even more worried.

'So stop panicking.' He shifted so he could whisper in her ear. 'I happen to *like* curves. You're all soft and feminine. Glorious. And you turn me on in a very big way. Remember what I said earlier tonight? "If ever any beauty I did see, Which I desired, and got, 'twas but a dream of thee."'

'What *is* that?' she asked.

'John Donne, a poem called "The Good-Morrow",' Max said. 'I studied his poetry for A level.'

'Ah.' She looked embarrassed. ' I've never read poetry, apart from the bits we did at school for GCSE. I stayed with maths, further maths, economics and physics for A level. But I'm not a total Philistine,' she added swiftly, clearly not wanting him to think badly of her. 'Lisa's taught me a lot about the theatre.'

He grinned. 'Good. That means I get the fun of teaching you about poetry. Especially Donne.'

Her brow furrowed. 'What's so special about Donne?'

'He married the woman he loved, when she was seventeen—in secret and against the wishes of her father—and he stayed with her, despite the fact it ruined his political career and it took her father nearly a decade to accept the marriage. And he wrote the most incredible poetry. His love poems are almost religious, and his religious poems are definitely love poems, too.'

'Right.'

She clearly wasn't any the wiser; so she really *didn't* know anything about poetry. He leaned forward to whisper in her ear. 'There's one where he talks about his mistress undressing. He only talks about her clothes, but you can tell just how much he wants her.' Just as much as he wanted Cyn. And one night he was going to get her to undress for him, and recite the poem to her as she undressed. Bit by bit.

The thoughts that evoked were enough to blow the rest of his common sense away. He brushed her earlobe with his lips. '"License my roving hands, and let them go, Before, behind, between, above, below,"' he whispered. Just what he'd started to do on the Embankment. What he'd wanted to do at the tube station. What he wanted to do right now.

Her eyes widened. 'Max!'

Shocked, perhaps—but she didn't move away. And there was a glimmer of desire in her eyes, too: the idea of him touching her all over turned her on. So the reality was going to blow both their minds. He gave her a lazy grin. 'That's just a foretaste.' Of the poem—and of what he wanted to do with her.

He wanted her naked.

In his bed.

And he wanted her there for a long, long time. So he could explore every inch of her. So he could find out exactly where and how she liked being touched, where and how she liked being kissed. And how her body would feel round his when she came. Repeatedly.

When they left the train, Cyn began to think that Max had some kind of sixth sense. Every time he realised that she was starting to think, to worry about how reckless she was being by going home with him tonight, he spun her into his arms and stole a kiss. And every time his mouth touched hers, her brain cells scrambled again.

She had no idea which roads they walked down or how long it took them to walk to his flat. Flat? It was a three-storey eighteenth-century townhouse. Then she remembered Lisa telling her that the ground floor of the building was his office and he lived on the top two floors.

The entrance hall was light and airy, painted a pale shade of aqua, with high ceilings and huge sash windows; there were intricate mouldings around the cornices and ceiling rose. The polished parquet flooring—the original, or at least an extremely accurate reproduction, she guessed—was set off by a rug in tones of aqua and cream.

'Wow,' she said.

He beamed, clearly pleased by her reaction. 'Like it?'

'It's fabulous,' she said honestly. 'I can see why Lisa loves working here—she said it had a lot more character than the modern office block she worked in with me. Is the rest of the place like this?'

'It is now. When I first saw the house, it was riddled with woodworm, the walls were cracked, the plaster was flaking off, the ceilings were a mess and the windows were rotting. It needed a lot of TLC—*and* it was a bit out of my price bracket, despite being in that sort of state. But I fell in love with it. Love at first sight. I just knew this was where I wanted to be. Where I *needed* to be.' He shrugged. 'So it was either keep my flat and find myself an office I could afford and try to forget my dreams, or sell the flat and sweet-talk my bank manager into giving me just a little bit more money, and rough it upstairs until I'd finished renovating this place. Until it looked the way I saw it in my head when everyone else was looking at a pile of rubble.'

It had been an easy choice for him, she could tell. And his face showed that he was still in love with the building. She remembered what he'd told her about the first building he'd ever worked on; and she'd bet that this house had been just as much a labour of love for him.

'How long did it take?'

'A couple of years. Every spare second I had, as well as ones I wasn't supposed to have.' He grinned. 'I got my friends to come here and help me paint walls in exchange for me cooking them dinner. My social life consisted of painting parties for about six months.' He paused. 'Which reminds me. We left the party early tonight. Did you have the chance to eat anything, or are you hungry?'

Cyn hadn't bothered having dinner first or nibbled at the canapés in the gallery. She'd been too keyed-up to eat. Still was. 'I'm fine.'

'Good,' he said, lifting her left hand to his mouth and kissing each finger in turn. 'Because food's the last thing on my mind. And although I'll give you a guided tour with pleasure, I'd rather it wasn't at this precise moment.' He shrugged off his coat and hung it on the post at the foot of the stairs, then removed her wrap and draped it over his coat. 'Right now,' he said softly, 'I want you. And nothing else but you.'

He bent his head and brushed his mouth over hers. The lightest, gentlest caress. Promising. Asking. And leaned back to wait for her response.

'Yes,' she said.

He pressed a kiss into her palm and folded her fingers over it.

'Take off your shoes,' he whispered.

She stepped out of them.

Then, to her shock, he picked her up. He cradled her in a way that meant she had to put her arms round his neck and hold on tightly, just as she had on the tube. And then he actually carried her up the stairs.

Any second now, she'd wake up and realise she'd just gone past her stop on the tube. That she'd been so tired, she'd fallen asleep and dreamed all this, just from catching that glimpse of Max at the party.

But then he kicked his bedroom door shut behind them. The sound was loud enough to make her realise this wasn't a dream. It was happening. Max Taylor had just carried her up the stairs to his bed.

And what a bed.

A polished cherrywood *bateau-lit*, definitely wider than the average bed. Soft, deep, fluffy-looking pillows. The pintucked duvet cover and bedlinen were pure white and perfectly smooth, with not even the hint of a crease.

Tomorrow morning, they'd be rumpled from a whole night of lovemaking.

Panic flared through her. Max was high maintenance. She'd bet that bed was either craftsman-made to order, or was a proper antique. Like the matching cheval-mirror, bedside cabinets and chest of drawers. This was way, way out of her comfort zone. Even the colour scheme was cool and urban and sophisticated, unlike the deep reds and old golds and terracotta shades she favoured. This was the house of a connoisseur. The floor was polished wood—and that was definitely real wood floor, not veneer—and the cream rug with a pattern that picked out the duck-egg blue of the walls looked as if it was silk.

Max let her slide down his body until her feet touched the floor—keeping her close, so she was in no doubt about how much he wanted her. Then he touched the base of the ceramic lamp to the left of the bed. Immediately, a soft glow lit the room. And then he closed the curtains—dark blue damask, which fell to the floor in soft pleats and shut out the sodium glow of the streetlights.

This was it. They were all alone. And it was too late to change her mind.

As if Max guessed what she was thinking, he walked back over to her and stood behind her, cradling her back against his body. 'It's okay,' he said softly. 'Don't worry about tomorrow. It's just another day. Lose yourself in me tonight.'

'I…' Her throat was so dry that her voice came out as a croak. And what on earth was she going to say, anyway? She couldn't exactly string a sentence together right now. Not when he was so close. Not when she could feel the heat of his body, smell his clean, citrus scent.

Gently, he turned her to face him. Touched his mouth lightly against hers. 'If you've changed your mind, I'll understand. I won't push you. But I think you want this as much as I do. *Need* this as much as I do.' He traced the outline of her face with his thumb. 'Be with me, Cyn. Let's forget the world outside. Right now it's just you and me and how we feel. Go with it. Make love with me.'

'Yes.'

It was the quietest whisper. For the space of a heartbeat, she didn't think he'd heard it. And then his hand reached behind her back to the top of her zip. Guided it slowly, slowly downwards. His fingertips brushed against her bare skin. 'So soft,' he murmured. 'I want to see you, Cyn. I want to touch you. All over.' He pushed the material of her dress from her shoulders and let it puddle to the floor.

Part of Cyn wanted to wrap her arms across her body, protect herself from his view. Yes, they'd slept together before. Yes, they'd made love together before—up to a point. But it had been in a darkened room. Here…there was light. Soft light, admittedly, but it was still light enough for him to see her exactly as she was. Which made her feel vulnerable. Exposed. Naked.

Scared.

He sucked in a breath. 'Oh, wow.'

He didn't sound as if he was regretting this. As if he wanted one of the tall, skinny blondes his type usually went for. His voice had grown deeper, huskier. 'Beautiful,' he breathed, drawing a finger along the lacy edge of her bra. 'And everything matches.'

Perfect grooming. High maintenance. Something she couldn't live up to, long term. Or even short term. Cyn was more comfortable with practical things. Business suits. No-nonsense underwear, not this frilly confection of lace. Things a world away from what a man like Max would want.

'You're thinking too much,' Max said, skimming his hands down her sides so they moulded to her curves. 'Stop listening to your head, Cyn. Listen to your body. Feel what I feel. Soft, soft skin. And the sharp contrast of the lace.' He brought his hands up again so that he cupped her breasts. 'It's slightly rough against my fingers.' His thumbs slid over her cleavage. 'Whereas here, you're so soft. Warm. Curvy. So very, very feminine. Just looking at you turns me on. I want to touch. I want to taste. I want *you*.'

She could feel her nipples hardening with anticipation. He was going to touch her. Maybe he'd make her wait. Maybe he'd make her ask him. But he was definitely going to touch her. Taste her. Take her to paradise and back.

'And here…' He circled her areola with the tip of his middle finger. 'Here the texture of your skin will be different.' There was just a thin layer of lace between his skin and hers, but it was still too much of a barrier for Cyn. The friction of the lace against her erect nipple was driving her crazy.

Perhaps she'd spoken aloud. Perhaps what she felt was obvious in her expression. But at last Max slid one hand round to her back and unsnapped the clasp of her bra. Let the black lace drop to the floor.

And then he wasn't smiling any more.

His face was intense. Yearning. Wanting. 'Beautiful,' he whispered, cupping her breasts and bending his head so the tip of his tongue teased her nipple.

Oh, Lord. He was good at this. So good. Cyn felt her knees buckle and gripped his shoulders for balance.

Max muttered something she didn't quite catch and lifted her. The next thing she knew, he'd pushed the duvet aside and she was lying on his bed, propped against the softest, plumpest pillows. Still keeping his gaze fixed on hers, Max slowly rolled down her hold-up stockings and dropped them on the floor beside the bed. He caressed every inch of skin as he revealed it, and Cyn discovered erogenous zones she hadn't even known she'd had. A sensitive spot at the back of her knee. The hollow of her anklebone. The soles of her feet, even: when Max touched her, every nerve end quivered with need and desire.

She arched back against the pillows, closing her eyes. She wanted a much, much deeper intimacy. Wanted his body to fill hers. Now.

And then she opened her eyes again as she felt Max's weight leave the bed. He was ripping off his clothes, clearly wanting exactly what she wanted and hardly able to wait.

The cashmere sweater hit the floor first. Lord, he was beautiful: perfect musculature, broad shoulders narrowing down to a neat waist, strong arms, long, narrow fingers, which could draw a plan in neat, meticulous detail—and which could also draw sheer pleasure from her body. She shivered in anticipation. Soon, she could touch him. Soon, he'd touch her again.

Soon, he'd be inside her.

She watched him unzip his trousers and push the material over his narrow hips. His jockey shorts and socks vanished at the same time—a man who knew that socks definitely weren't sexy, she thought with a grin.

But Lord, Lord, he was beautiful. Washboard stomach, a perfect bottom. And his sex…

Her mouth went dry.

Then his eyes caught hers and she forgot to breathe at all.

'We're equals, now,' Max said softly as he joined her on the bed. He hooked his thumbs into the waistband of her knickers. 'Well, nearly. And this is what I've wanted all evening. You, naked, in my bed.'

She tipped her head back against the pillows as he kissed his way down her body. Gentle pressure on her lower back made her lift her buttocks, and he peeled her knickers down. Baring her completely to him.

'"License my roving hands, and let them go, Before, behind, between, above, below,"' he murmured.

He wanted to touch her. All over. Was *going* to touch her all over. And she was near the point of hyperventilating. If he didn't do something to ease the ache soon, she was going to implode. She tilted her hips against him. 'You're driving me crazy,' she whispered.

'Good.'

Good?

'Now you know what it's like for me.'

He felt this same desperate need?

'I want you so much, it hurts,' he confirmed. 'I can't think straight. All I can see is you. All I can feel is you. And all I want to taste…' He leaned forward and circled her areola with his tongue. 'All I want to taste,' he whispered, 'is you.'

She was definitely hyperventilating, now. Her whole body was quivering. Wanting him. Wanting him to fill her and ease this desperate need. 'Now, Max,' she breathed. 'Please. Now.'

He leaned over her, removed a condom from the drawer and rolled it on. He knelt between her legs, and she closed her eyes.

'Don't close your eyes,' he said softly. 'I want to see you.'

See the look in her eyes. Read every thought in her head. So incredibly intimate. And when she opened her eyes again, all she could see was the desire in his eyes. Hot, smouldering desire. All for her.

She couldn't even remember the last time she'd done this with the light on, much less watched someone's face as they'd made love. This felt dangerous. But she couldn't stop. Not now. She wanted him too badly.

He slid one hand between her legs, cupping her. Teasing her. She wriggled, needing closer contact. Needing friction. Needing him to rub at the spot that ached for his touch.

His finger skated along her core, and her breath hissed.

'Okay?' he asked.

'No.'

His eyes widened. 'I'm sorry. I'll stop.'

'No!' She'd die if he stopped now.

He frowned, and then his mouth stretched in a lazy grin. 'So that first no was a yes, was it?'

'No, it was a no. As in I want…' Tell him. She had to tell him. She dragged in a breath. 'It wasn't okay because it wasn't enough. I want—I need—*more*.'

'Uh-huh. I think we'll have to work on your phraseology.' He slid one finger inside her, pushing deep. It was good. Good. But not enough.

'More,' she said again. 'Please. More.'

He bent his head, drew one nipple into his mouth. Sucked. Hard. She tipped her head back, thrusting her ribcage up. This was what she wanted...almost.

She tilted her pelvis so she rubbed herself against the base of his thumb, and rocked her hips.

'Better,' she said.

'Tell me what you want.'

It wasn't a demand. It was a plea. And she knew exactly what he wanted to hear. What she wanted to feel. What they both needed, right now. 'I want you inside me, Max. I want to feel you buried inside me. Deep as you can.' She sounded like a slut! Desperate.

But he didn't seem to mind.

In fact, he had the same slightly desperate look on his face. As if to say that if they didn't make love, right here, right now—all the way—he was going to implode.

Just as she would.

He shifted slightly, fitting himself against her entrance. Unable to stop herself, she pushed up to meet him, and he slid home.

At her sharp exhalation, he held himself tense. 'Do you want me to stop? Did I hurt you?'

He cared that much for her that he'd stop—leave himself frustrated rather than hurt her? She melted. 'No. It's just...been a while,' she admitted. 'And I want you too much.'

'Me, too, so I'm probably not going to last too long. It's not going to be as good as you deserve,' he warned. 'Not the first time, anyway.'

The first time? He was planning...more? The thought sent desire rocketing through her. She needed this. Right now. 'This feels good enough to me,' she said, and wrapped her legs round his waist.

He grinned. 'You wait. Because it's only going to get better, honey.'

Max wasn't her first lover, but she couldn't remember it ever being like this. The intense, raw desire in his eyes thrilled her. His body fitted hers perfectly, and his first shallow strokes had her quivering. And then, as he pushed deeper, driving into her, she felt herself soaring higher and higher.

This was exactly what she wanted. What she needed. What she'd been looking for, without really knowing it.

Just Max.

And the realisation almost stopped her breathing. Max was The One. He couldn't be. Logically, he couldn't be—he was everything she should avoid. A playboy. A man who couldn't commit. A man who'd break her heart.

But he was everything she wanted. Clever. Driven. Passionate. A man who took risks and followed his heart. A man who turned her on with a single look—and whose company didn't bore her.

Max was The One.

He couldn't be. They barely knew each other. It was way too soon.

And yet…she knew.

She closed her eyes, and he stopped moving.

Shocked, she opened her eyes and stared at him. 'Max?'

'Better.' His eyes were hot and feral. 'Much better.' He stole a kiss. 'Don't close your eyes. I want to see you, Cyn. I want to see your eyes when you come.'

This was much, much more than she'd expected. Especially when he began to move again. Slow, shallow strokes that had her quivering. And then deeper, deeper. As she felt his body shudder against hers she looked deep into his eyes. Saw the need and the burning hunger there. Mirrored from her own gaze.

And her body tightened round his.

CHAPTER THIRTEEN

THE next morning, Cyn woke, feeling warm and comfortable and very much at peace with the world. If there was such a thing as perfection, this was it. Waking up in bed with Max Taylor. He was curled behind her, spooned against her, his arm wrapped tightly round her and holding her to him.

She'd spent the night with him, in his enormous *bateau-lit*. And what a night. Max had taken her to paradise and back. Several times. She was definitely sleep deprived, but she wouldn't have missed a single moment of last night. The way he'd made her feel. The way he'd pushed back all the barriers so in the end there were only the two of them, skin to skin, and nothing else mattered.

Now, it was late enough for morning light to be filtering through into the room. Which meant she had to make a decision: stay or go?

Her body screamed that it wanted to stay exactly where it was, wrapped in Max's arms.

Her mind knew that wasn't a good idea. Because what had last night really been about, to Max? Sex. Very good sex, admittedly—but still just sex. He hadn't said a word to her about love.

Not that she expected him to. They hadn't known each other that long. Logically, he couldn't possibly have fallen in love with her. Even though she knew now she'd fallen for him. In the light of morning, Cyn's mind had switched back to logical mode, and she was sensible enough to know it wouldn't work out between them. She'd seen this happen so many times before with her mother. And she'd chosen exactly the same kind of man for herself: one who didn't want to settle down. Today, Max would start to think about the possibility of emotional commitment and Cyn knew he'd panic. This was too soon, too fast, too much. He'd already told her he didn't do commitment. Lisa had told her that he didn't date women more than three times, and Cyn really didn't want to end up eating her heart out over him.

So it was better to leave now—now, before the huge crack in the middle of her heart split open and reduced her to rubble. Carefully, gently, she prised his arm away. Slipped out from the covers. And she was just about to hunt down her clothes when his voice stopped her.

'Where are you going?'

He was *awake*?

'Come back to bed.' It was an invitation, not an order. A soft, sleepy, *sexy* invitation.

One she wanted to accept. And one she really had to refuse, for her own peace of mind. She kept her back to him. 'I need to be in the office this morning. Catch up on all the stuff I didn't have a chance to do in the week when I was troubleshooting for the Wharf Gallery.' Though she'd have to go home first and change. *And* face Lisa. She wasn't looking forward to that and the explanations her extremely nosy housemate would demand.

'Cyn. Look at me.'

She did. Mistake. He looked rumpled and sexy and utterly desirable, and she was within a hair's breadth of leaping straight back into his bed.

'Do you *really* have to go?'

Not for work. But for the sake of her sanity. She nodded.

'Stay a bit longer,' he invited. 'You're going to get very cold standing there.'

Cold was good. Cold meant her brain would work. If she climbed back into bed with him, her brain would turn back into a pile of mush.

'Plus—' his voice deepened '—I can't concentrate when you're naked and right in my line of vision. You're too distracting.'

Oh, God. How could she possibly have forgotten that she was naked?

But Max did that to her. When she was near him, she forgot about everything except him. Which scared the hell out of her. She hated that feeling of not being in control.

'I'm not going to leap on you. Even though I admit that I want to.' He shifted to the side, pulled the duvet back and patted the mattress. 'Come and talk to me.'

Even knowing that it wasn't a good idea, she couldn't resist the mute appeal in his eyes. How could blue eyes possibly have the same effect on you as a pair of soulful brown spaniel's eyes? It wasn't logical. But Max's did.

Silently, she climbed into the bed and covered herself with the duvet, though she made sure she wasn't sitting too close to him.

Max reached out to tangle his fingers with hers. 'Tell me what's wrong, honey,' he said softly.

She'd bet he called *all* his women 'honey'. Time to face facts. She was just one of a long, long line. And there would be plenty more after her. 'Last night…' Oh, how could she put this without sounding pathetic?

'Last night was good.' He raised her hand to his mouth. 'If it wasn't good for you, all you had to do was tell me what you wanted. Teach me what you like. Show me where you wanted me to touch you—*how* you wanted me to touch you.'

Cyn felt the colour rush into her face. 'I didn't mean that.'

'I'm glad.' Though he didn't sound puffed-up with pride; it wasn't an ego thing, then.

'Because I wanted last night to be good for you, too,' he added softly.

It had been. But… This was today. This was reality. 'I don't do flings, Max. I've seen what they did to my mum.'

He frowned. 'I don't understand.'

'My mum…everyone looked down on us in the village. You saw that at the wedding. I wanted to show them all that I was as good as them—no, better.'

'Because you were the scholarship kid, not from a rich family?'

'Partly. And partly—' she lifted her chin '—because I didn't have a dad.' Her eyes blazed at him, daring him to say she wasn't good enough for him because she was illegitimate.

Max knew he had to make sure he said the right thing. The problem was, he didn't know what to say. He didn't want to hurt her, add another layer to past hurts. But he couldn't promise her for ever, either; he wasn't a for ever kind of man. And this was rapidly becoming the worst morning-after awkwardness he'd ever experienced. 'Does it matter that you didn't have a dad?' he asked at last.

The tension in her face relaxed, just a tiny bit. 'It did to everyone else in the village. I wanted to prove that my mum didn't make a mistake in keeping me.'

Cyn thought she was a *mistake*? He squeezed her hand. 'I've met your mother, remember. I've seen how she is with you. She loves you. And she's very, very proud of you. I very much doubt she ever thought you were a mistake.'

'*She* didn't.' Cyn swallowed miserably. 'Other people did. That she shouldn't have kept me because I held her back. I don't know how, but Michelle Wilson found out about my dad. She told everyone. The whispers in the playground, the little looks... I hated it. But what I really minded was what they said about my mum. She wasn't a tart.'

'Of course your mother isn't a tart!' Max frowned. 'Why on earth did they say that?'

'Because she had a few—' She broke off and shook her head. 'A few? More like a lot of relationships. All short-lived. She was looking for Mr Right. Which wasn't my father, because...' She sucked in a breath, her face a mask of misery.

'Because?' Max prompted gently.

'Because he was already married,' she whispered. 'Mum had no idea, or she'd never have gone anywhere near him. She only found out when she was pregnant— and then he told her why he couldn't possibly marry her. He already had a wife. My mum was just...a diversion.'

Max stared at her in disbelief. 'What a bastard.'

'She broke it off, that night. Didn't see him again. She told him about me when I was born—even though he'd treated her badly, she thought he had a right to know that he had a daughter. He wrote back and said he didn't want anything to do with us, and sent her a cheque. A large cheque—I suppose it was his way of dealing with things. Chuck money at a problem and it'll go away.' A muscle flickered in her jaw. 'My mother ripped the cheque in half and returned it to him. Without a note.'

'She's a strong woman,' Max said softly. 'Like you.'

And this told him exactly why Cyn had issues with relationships. The first man in her life—the man she should have been able to trust to stand by her, come hell or high water—had rejected her. No wonder she didn't believe that any man would offer her commitment.

He shifted uncomfortably. And, considering how bad he was on the commitment front himself, she definitely wouldn't believe he would offer her what she wanted. He wasn't too sure that he could, either. He'd failed with Gina. And he sure as hell didn't want to hurt Cyn the same way. 'Has your dad tried to contact you since?' Max asked.

'No. I know who he is—Mum never kept it a secret from me. She said if I wanted to contact him, she'd help me. But he's never been interested in knowing anything about his daughter—and I really don't think I want to know him. Would you believe, he's on his fourth wife, and she's about three years younger than I am?' Cyn pulled a face. 'I think he trades them in for a younger model, every five to ten years.'

So Cyn thought that would happen to her? Or—worse—was she saying she thought *he* was like that? 'Not all men are like your father,' he said quietly.

'I know.' She stared at the crumpled duvet cover. Crumples they had made. 'But Mum's never met the right man for her. I've heard her crying herself to sleep too many times after she's been let down by the one she thought was Mr Right, and he turned out to be Mr Right Now.'

'You're not your mother.'

Cyn stared at him in seeming dislike. 'I couldn't have had a better mother.'

No, no, she'd got him wrong. 'I wasn't saying she's a bad mother or anything like that, Cyn. For your information, when I met her, I liked her. A lot. All I'm saying is that you're different people. Just because your mum never found the right one for her, it doesn't mean that you won't find the right one for you.'

'I don't want to make the same mistakes she has and pin all my hopes on a relationship that isn't going to work.' Cyn shrugged. 'You and I—we're too different. As I said, I don't do flings. And I know you don't do commitment. So maybe we should just say goodbye now.'

Oh, hell. She'd laid it right on the line. She wasn't prepared to see where this was going to take them. She'd already made up her mind that he was Mr Wrong—and she was going to walk away.

The problem was, Max didn't *want* her to walk away.

But he couldn't promise her for ever, either.

Because, although he thought she really could be The One, he'd made that mistake before. Hurt someone he'd really cared about. And he didn't want the same thing to happen with Cyn.

'Cyn. I don't… Look, I'm not good at this sort of thing. I told you about what happened with Gina. I admit that I've made a mess of serious relationships, in the past— that's why I…' No. It definitely wouldn't be a good idea to tell her about the fact he rarely dated the same woman more than two or three times. Apart from being tactless, it would send her running out of his bed. And he wanted her to stay. He sighed. 'I just don't want you to walk out of my life.'

'So what do you want, Max?'

If she'd asked him that last night, his answer would have been simple. *I want to be the best at what I do. I want to restore houses—restore them well enough to gain respect from everyone in my field, and win awards.*

Now… He still wanted that. But did he want more?

He'd already tried that with Gina. Tried and failed. Gina was like Cyn: sweet, a little shy—in short, a nice girl. Max didn't date nice girls any more. He only went out with women who played as hard as he did. Women who knew the rules.

If he took things further with Cyn, he'd have to remake the rules. And he wasn't quite sure what that would do to the balance of his world.

'See? You can't answer me,' she said quietly.

He gave her the answer he'd prepared earlier. 'I want to be the best at what I do.'

'But what about on a personal level?'

'What do *you* want?' he fenced.

She was silent for a long, long moment. And then she exhaled sharply. 'I don't know, either.'

'Maybe we should sleep on it.'

'Meaning you want to have sex.'

'No.'

Why was she looking insulted when he'd just said he hadn't meant sex? Then the penny dropped. 'I mean, yes. Of course I want to have sex with you. Didn't last night show you just how attractive I find you? But I didn't mean that was *all* I wanted.' He shook his head in frustration. 'Don't twist my words, Cyn.'

'I have to go to work.'

Letting her run out now would be a mistake. He knew that. But if she stayed, things were only going to get more awkward. Boxed in. Which wasn't fair to either of them. Maybe they needed space between them to work this out.

'Okay. You have stuff to do, and I have to prepare for a site meeting.' He paused. 'But I'll call you.'

'You'll call me.' She looked as if she'd heard that one before—and she didn't believe a word of it.

'Really.' He meant it. He didn't want her to walk out of his life. 'Give me your mobile number. I'll call you.'

'All right. Got a pen?'

He kept one in his bedside cabinet, to do the crossword

in the Sunday papers. Without a word, he took it from the drawer and handed it to her.

'Paper?'

'Not here. I'll have to go down to my office.'

To his surprise, she shook her head. 'This'll do.' She took his hand and scrawled her phone number on the back.

Now *that* was thinking on her feet. And Max liked that. He liked that a lot.

Actually, there were a lot of things he liked about Cynthia Reynolds. He just hoped she'd give him the chance to tell her. 'I'll call you,' he promised.

And he meant to. He really did. He even transferred her number to his mobile phone before he showered and scrubbed the ink from his hand. Except his muse took him over partway through his preparations for the site meeting, and he only realised he'd forgotten about both lunch and dinner when he'd finished roughing out some sketches on his draughtboard and noticed that it was dark outside.

It was nearly ten o'clock at night. Hardly a reasonable time to call her. For all he knew, she was out somewhere—after all, this was Saturday night. A night when he'd usually be out partying. He'd just been…distracted, today. Well, he hadn't said *when* he'd call. He'd ring her tomorrow. At a reasonable hour.

He tried. Except he kept hearing the network message that the mobile phone he was calling was unavailable. So she must be on the tube or some other place where there wasn't a phone signal.

He thought about sending a text—but somehow it didn't seem quite right. Impersonal. A bit like an after-thought. Anyway, he wanted to talk to her.

Ah, hell. If he'd called her yesterday, they could've spent today together. Maybe gone down to Kew, wandered through the gardens. He could have kissed her in every greenhouse—in fact, in one, he could have kissed her in several different climates. Hot and dry. Cool and humid.

Mmm, and if they'd found a quiet corner, hot and wet...

He tried again later, but this time the recorded message told him that her mobile phone was switched off.

Okay. He'd try her landline. He knew the number because Lisa shared it.

But the line was engaged and she didn't have an answering service that took a message when she was on the phone or using the Internet.

Why the hell didn't a techie have broadband, to keep her phone line free and give her faster net access?

He growled in frustration when he tried again a few minutes later and got the engaged signal yet again. Anyone would think Cyn was trying to avoid him. She certainly wasn't making it easy for him to contact her.

Unless, maybe, she'd changed her mind and didn't want him to call her...

I'll call you.

Yeah, right. Cyn had left her mobile phone on virtually all weekend, and Max hadn't called. Okay, so some of the time she'd been travelling and there hadn't been a signal, but he could have texted her and she'd have picked up the message when she was back in an area with a signal. Or he could have emailed her. She'd told him she'd be in the office.

She'd had the best part of two days to think about it. A relationship with Max—well, it wouldn't be a relationship, would it? It would be a couple of dates, and then it would be over. He didn't do commitment. He'd been honest with her, even telling her about Gina.

But it had also been a warning. He'd told her that Gina

was quiet and shy—and not what he wanted. She knew from Lisa that Max dated tall, skinny blondes who were happy to party hard for just a little while and then wave him goodbye. Tall, skinny, fancy-free blondes. The opposite of short, curvy, intense brunettes. Ha.

That left her two options. One, do what her mum did and eat her heart out over Mr Wrong. Two, get real—Max Taylor wasn't going to give up his single lifestyle and risk a proper relationship. So she'd be better off just leaving it and moving on.

Wouldn't she?

The next morning, Cyn was about to head into a meeting when her mobile phone rang.

'Hey. You're a hard woman to get hold of, Cyn Reynolds.'

Oh, Lord. Even Max's voice made her melt. Made her body remember how it had felt to be stroked, kissed, all over. Cyn closed her eyes. No. She'd made her decision. And she wasn't going to change it. No matter how seductive he sounded.

'Not that difficult,' she said coolly.

'I got caught up in work on Saturday,' Max said. 'I didn't think you'd appreciate a call at stupid o'clock.'

True. But he could have texted her.

'Your phone wasn't available yesterday. And your landline was busy.'

He'd tried to call her? Really? 'I was working.'

'I guessed as much. Can I see you for lunch?'

Oh, yes, please. Especially if you're on the menu.

She shook herself. No. She'd made her choice. It was time to be sensible. 'Sorry. I'm working.'

'Dinner tonight, then.'

It wouldn't be just dinner, would it? She remembered

what he'd said on Friday night. *Come home with me.* He'd say the same to her tonight. She, being stupid, wouldn't have the slightest bit of resistance. She'd go. Willingly. And they'd have another night of amazing sex.

Until he got bored.

Or until he got spooked. Three dates and she'd be out. Which meant tonight would be their last time together in any case. What was the point of setting herself up for getting hurt? 'Sorry. I'm working.' Not quite as unsubtle as 'I'm washing my hair', but he'd get the message. 'And I'm due in a meeting right now. Bye.' She pressed the button to end the call, then switched off her phone.

Max swore as he heard the long beeping tone, and cleared the line. She'd hung up on him! He pressed 'redial'—and discovered that, not only had she hung up on him, she'd switched off her phone.

Oh, wonderful. Not. Clearly she'd thought about it over the weekend, panicked, and decided not to give them a chance.

Ah, hell. He didn't know where they were going, either. He couldn't give her any promises because he had no idea what was happening between them. Normally, he managed to walk away without a problem. But Cyn was different. He wasn't going to leave it at this. He *couldn't*. There was something about her—something that made him want to get to know her better. Made him want to spend time with her. Made him want to break his personal rule of not letting a woman get too close to him. Cyn *mattered*.

So. Should he send her flowers? No, too obvious. If he was going to sweet-talk Cyn into giving them a chance…

Sweet-talk. Of course.

He grinned, and flicked into his Internet browser.

Fifteen minutes later he'd chosen a selection of very exclusive chocolates, added a very personal message and booked them to be couriered to her that afternoon.

Cyn came out of her third meeting of the afternoon to find a gold-coloured box on her desk.

She frowned. 'What are these?' she asked Rob.

Her colleague looked up from his desk and shrugged. 'Delivered for you when you were in that meeting.'

Odd. She wasn't expecting anything. It wasn't her birthday. She opened the box, and her eyes widened when she saw the chocolates. Wow. Really top-quality stuff, from the best chocolatier in London.

Maybe it was from the Wharf Gallery, to say thank you. Sweet. She'd share it with the guys—after all, they'd put in the hours as well. She smiled, opened the envelope and read the card.

Colour scorched into her cheeks. Max had sent her chocolates. Just as she'd sent them to him. And he'd talked about wanting to eat chocolate off her skin.

The man was trying to seduce her with chocolate.

The worst thing was, she could just imagine it. And her libido was already starting to sit up and beg.

'Everything all right, Cyn?' Rob asked.

'Uh, yes.' No.

She flicked into her email program and typed a quick note. Three seconds later, she'd pulled Max's email address from her files and sent the message.

She was working on debugging a program when her computer beeped.

Mail.

Knowing she should just ignore it—but unable to stop herself—she checked her inbox. One new message, from Max Taylor.

No offence meant. Have dinner with me. Tonight. My place. I'll cook for you. M.

Dinner at his place? Yeah, right. She'd never even make it to his kitchen! They'd end up in his bed. And she'd end up hurt. She pressed 'reply' and typed.

Thanks, but no. C.

Beep.

In case you're worried about food poisoning, I love cooking—and I'm *good* at things I love doing. M.

Like sex.
She already knew that.
And she knew he knew she'd think of that.
Ah, hell. She ate a chocolate. And that reminded her of sex, too, because of that little picture he'd put in her mind. Sex and chocolate. Was she ever going to be able to eat chocolate again without thinking of him? Without thinking of making love? Damn. She pressed 'reply' and typed.

The answer's still no.

Two seconds later, her office phone rang. She picked it up almost on automatic pilot. 'Good afternoon, Cyn Reynolds speaking.'

'I'll do you coffee ice cream and strawberries for dessert.'

He didn't even need to give his name. She knew his voice. And she knew what he was trying to do. Put more pictures in her mind. Tempting pictures. Of Max feeding her spoonfuls of ice cream between kisses. Of him offering her a plump, juicy strawberry to take a bite. Of being stretched out on his lovely big bed, while he...

She took a deep breath. 'Max, I'm about to go into a meeting.'

'Another one?' He sounded disbelieving. Well, she never had been good at lying.

'I'm busy.'

He didn't dispute that. But his voice became softer, coaxing. 'Talk to me, Cyn. Give me a chance.'

So tempting. But she couldn't do it. 'No.'

'Why?'

'Because you'll hurt me, Max. And I don't want to get hurt.' Before he could say anything else, she said, 'Good-bye.' And hung up.

That was twice she'd hung up on him. Twice more than any other woman had before. With any other woman, he'd have shrugged and walked away. No hard feelings. But, with Cyn, he couldn't.

Which was precisely why he ought to stay away from her. She'd change everything. And he liked his life as it was—working hard and playing harder.

But he remembered waking up with her in his arms. Once most definitely wasn't enough.

Okay, so the chocolates hadn't worked. But he was going to wear her resistance down. And how.

He flicked back into the Internet. Scrolled through flowers that just wouldn't work. Cyn wasn't a red roses girl—besides, red roses were way too obvious. He wanted something cool and beautiful. Was there a flower called Cinderella?

Yes. Snapdragons with pink and pale shell-pink flowers—which flowered from June, so they were well out of season. Or delphiniums with pale violet-coloured flowers—again, out of season. Ditto the clematis with blue flowers. Ha. Served him right for trying to be too clever.

In the end he chose an arrangement of spectacular scented lilies and white roses. Something cool and beautiful, like Cyn herself. He ordered special delivery for first thing tomorrow morning, and added a message he hoped would intrigue Cyn enough to make her call him.

And waited for the reaction.

It was the middle of Tuesday afternoon when she finally emailed him. And that was when Max realised that he really *had* been waiting to hear from her. He hadn't been giving his full attention to the project he was working on, so he'd need to double-check every single calculation.

Something else he'd never had to do before.

He clicked on the message.

Thank you for the flowers. They're lovely. But do you have any idea how much teasing I've had to take from my team over this?

It hadn't even occurred to him that she'd be teased. But, now he thought of it, she worked with a bunch of male techies. Of course they would have ribbed her when flowers arrived. It was a guy thing. Ask her who her secret admirer was and watch her blush.

Quickly, he typed back.

Sorry. That wasn't meant to happen. I just hoped you'd like them. Have dinner with me tonight?

The reply was too fast and too brief.

No.

Because she was still scared he'd hurt her?

He was going to have to address the issue. Starting now.

There are no guarantees this is all going to end in tears.

There are no guarantees it *won't*.

Ah, he'd had enough of this. Email was too distant. And he knew she was at her desk right this very moment. He dialled her direct line without looking it up—funny, he hadn't even realised he'd memorised it from the bottom of her email signature—and scowled as he got her voice-mail.

He waited for the beep. 'Cyn. I know you're there. Be brave. Take a risk. Call me.'

He just hoped she would.

CHAPTER FOURTEEN

SHE didn't.

And he couldn't leave it.

So, on Wednesday, Max sent Cyn a poem: Donne's 'The Good-Morrow'—the poem he'd quoted to her on the train; the poem he'd quoted the night they'd made love.

No response.

On Thursday, he hand-delivered a small package to her office. A CD containing the track the busker had played in the tube station, the night he'd kissed her by the Thames. With a handwritten note.

Still no response.

On the Friday, Max intended to go over to Cyn's office and talk her into having lunch with him. Even if it was only a quick sandwich in the local deli. He just wanted to see her. Talk to her. Persuade her to give him a chance— because she'd got under his skin more than any other woman he'd known. It wasn't the thrill of the chase. It was…something else. Something that he didn't want to analyse too closely in case it really was the L-word, the thing he'd been avoiding for years.

But then Lisa brought in his mail and all hell broke loose.

Max read through the letter and slammed it down on

his desk in disbelief. This was outrageous. Of *course* he hadn't submitted someone else's designs in the competition he'd entered a couple of months ago! There must have been a mistake. Some kind of admin mix-up. He'd never even *heard* of Jason Henry.

He managed to hold onto his temper—just—and rang the organiser. When he finally replaced the receiver, he was ready to throw something small and heavy through a very large plate-glass window.

He had not stolen someone else's designs. And he could prove it. He'd kept a copy of his entry; all he had to do was duplicate it and courier it over. Proof that it was their mistake. He wasn't a cheat. He didn't need to cheat!

He stomped over to his filing cabinet, yanked out the drawer, and looked for the competition file.

Nothing.

Maybe he'd misfiled it. Or Lisa had misfiled it. But it wasn't in the drawer where it should have been. Or in any of the other three drawers he kept for current work.

Okay, it was an easy mistake to make when you were busy; he must have just put it in the wrong cabinet.

But it wasn't under C in any of the other cabinets, either.

He strode out of his office. 'Have you seen the file for my competition entry?' he asked.

'In your filing cabinet, under C,' Lisa said, without looking up from her screen. 'They're in alpha order, so try under COM.'

'It's not there.'

She must have heard the suppressed panic in his voice because, this time, she looked at him. 'Maybe you put it back in the wrong place.'

'I've just been through the entire "current" filing cabinet. And the C drawer for past clients, just in case. It isn't there.'

'Okay. I'll have a look.' She frowned. 'What's up?'

'Apparently, the design I submitted is the same as another architect's. And his firm is claiming that I stole his design.'

'That's ridiculous. You wouldn't do anything like that.'

'I'm a little fish and they're a whale. Who are you going to believe?'

'You, of course. It's just a stupid admin mix-up. As soon as we get the originals over to them, they'll see it's their mistake and they'll grovel abjectly at your feet.'

Her loyalty and trust in him made him feel slightly better. But unfortunately hers wasn't the view that would matter most. 'Slight problem. I can't find the bloody design. And if I can't prove it's mine, I'll be disqualified.' Not to mention having a huge stain on his reputation. A stain that would never go away. A stain that would stop people asking him to tender for restoration jobs—because the suspicion would always be there. Had he cheated or hadn't he? Was he reliable or wasn't he? Could they trust him or couldn't they?

Crashed and burned. Everything he'd worked for, turned to ashes. It didn't bear thinking about.

'You didn't chuck it out when you had your big decluttering session, a couple of months back?' Lisa suggested.

'Of course not.' Though he was even less certain than he knew he sounded. *Could* he have done something that stupid—thrown away a file by mistake?

'Well, at least you've got the computer files,' she said comfortingly. 'They'll prove your innocence.'

He hoped so.

But when he switched the computer on, he couldn't find the files. Anywhere. They'd just vanished—along with what looked like most of the contents of his computer. There certainly wasn't a program where he could look up his files. 'Oh, my God. What's happened?' he asked in dismay.

Lisa took a look. 'I think your computer just got fried. Didn't you have the anti-virus thingy on?'

'Yes, of course I did. And it checks for updates automatically every morning.' He swallowed sickly. 'I hope to hell I can get those files back. I'd better ring the dealer.'

'I'll do it.' But when Lisa came back into his office, Max knew from her expression what she was going to say.

'Just give me the bad news,' he said.

'They're stacked up. They can't help until next Wednesday at the earliest.'

Max grabbed a handful of his hair and pulled hard. Nope, it wasn't a nightmare. It hurt, therefore this was really happening. 'I don't believe this. What the hell am I going to do? If I can't prove that design is mine, I'll be disqualified. That's my reputation gone—because mud sticks. And, without a reputation, I won't have a business for much longer. I'm already losing clients as it is.' And was that connected? He hadn't seen the link before. Had his lost clients gone to Jason Henry? Had Jason Henry been the one to copy his designs for the Watkins property? Max would have to check. Dig deeper, if he had to. And then he'd act.

He shook his head. 'I can't wait until next Wednesday. I need to sort this now.' Now, before rumours started spreading.

What he needed was someone who was brilliant with computers. Someone who loved troubleshooting. And he knew just the person—except, right now, Cyn wasn't exactly speaking to him.

Ah, hell. How could he possibly ask her?

But if he didn't, he could lose everything. His throat felt so full, he could barely breathe. Time to swallow his pride.

Ask for her help. And hope that she didn't say no—that she didn't think he was just using her. 'I'm going to make a phone call,' he said, and left the office before Lisa had the chance to say anything.

Cyn reread the letter for the third time, hoping she'd completely misread it. But no, it was all there in black and white. The job had gone to an external candidate. She was going to have to work for someone else—someone who'd got *her* job. But the bit that really stuck in her craw was the comment that the interviewers felt she put too many hours in and they were looking for someone with a more rounded social profile.

How the hell could you put *too many* hours in at work? They'd asked her to do it, in the first place! It just wasn't fair to ask someone to do you a favour—then slam them for doing it. If she'd said no, worked her set hours, they'd have labelled her a clock watcher. She'd said yes, and they'd stuck a different label on her—but one that was just as damaging.

And what was a 'more rounded social profile' anyway? Someone who was happy to sit in the pub and talk shop? Someone who leaped at the idea of those outdoor team-building training courses where you had to abseil down cliffs and trust people in your team to catch you when you fell backwards?

When her phone rang, Cyn was tempted to let it go through to her voicemail. But maybe keeping herself busy was the best way of dealing with her disappointment. She picked up the receiver. 'Cyn Reynolds.' No cheery 'good morning' from her today. Because it wasn't a good morning. At all. The only saving grace was that it was Friday. And as she supposedly worked flexible hours, she'd be out of RCS on the dot of half past three.

'Cyn, thank God you're there.' He paused. 'It's Max.'

As if she hadn't recognised his voice. 'Oh.'

He must have heard the wariness in her tone because his voice sharpened. 'Look, I'm not going to hassle you about us.'

What us? There was no 'us'!

'I just…' He sucked in a breath. 'You're busy, so I'll cut to the chase. I'm in a mess. A real mess. My computer's fried.'

'That's what dealers are for,' Cyn pointed out. 'You have a maintenance contract, don't you?'

'Yes, but they can't do it in time. I need help now, not next week.'

Cyn had heard this kind of story so many times before. 'Then check the backup disks. You do keep backups, I assume?' Though they probably weren't up to date. She knew from experience that it always took a virus attack to make people keep proper daily backups, and even then the habit rarely lasted more than a fortnight.

'Cyn, I wouldn't be calling you if I wasn't desperate.'

'Uh-huh.'

He groaned. 'That didn't come out right. I meant, this is business. And I know you're busy. And I'll pay for your time. And…I just need help. Fast. From the best.'

He thought she was the best in her field? And, from the desperation in his voice, he wasn't flattering her. He really had called her because he needed a computer systems troubleshooter—someone who would do the job fast, and do it brilliantly. A warm glow started somewhere in the region of her heart. 'What's happened?' she asked.

'I've been accused of stealing someone else's designs.'

'What?' Max might be untrustworthy where her heart was concerned, but in other respects he had more integrity than any other man she'd ever met. 'Sounds as if you need a lawyer, not a techie.'

'Later, maybe. But not right now. Look, my paper-work's vanished. I have files on my computer, but if I can't retrieve them I can't prove anything. If my reputa-tion goes, so does my business. I need to prove I'm innocent. Can you help me? Please?'

You owe me a favour, Cyn Reynolds. And I'll collect... some time.

The memory sent a shiver through Cyn, and she hastily pushed it out of her mind. This was a work favour—and it would more than repay what he'd done for her. And, right now, Cyn didn't want to be at RCS anyway. 'All right. I'm owed some time.' Which was putting it mildly. If she took all the time she was owed, they'd have to find themselves another lead programmer for the next six months. 'Don't turn the computer off. I'm on my way.'

'You're a star.' Max gave her rapid directions to his office from Bayswater Tube station.

Just as well. She couldn't remember the way. Not after—no, she wasn't going to think about that night. About how he'd kissed her all the way home.

'I'll have coffee waiting for you,' he promised.

'No worries.'

'And, Cyn?'

'Yes?'

'Thank you,' he said softly. 'I mean it. I really appre-ciate this.'

Cyn replaced the receiver and slipped her utilities disks into a carry-case. 'I'm taking some time in lieu,' she said to Rob. 'I'll ring in later and tell you how long I'll be.'

'What? But you never take time in lieu,' Rob said, looking surprised.

'I do now.' She gave him a tight smile. If she wasn't good enough for the promotion, she also wasn't good enough to work for more hours than she was contracted to work. And her employers were the ones who said she put too many hours in. QED. She was taking time off and there was absolutely nothing they could say about it. 'If anyone wants me…' She shrugged. 'Well, they'll just have to wait, won't they?'

Ignoring the shock on Rob's face, she switched off her computer, took her handbag from her desk drawer and the laptop case from under her desk, and walked out of the office.

The nearer Cyn got to Bayswater, the faster her heart was beating. Every stop on the tube raised her pulse a notch. Adrenaline tingled at the back of her neck and the tips of her fingers. She was going to see Max again. The man who'd sent her exceptional chocolate. The man who'd quoted poetry to her. The man who'd kissed her on the bank of the Thames and sent her into such a whirl she'd forgotten where she was.

The man she'd turned down, because she didn't want her heart broken.

Then a really nasty thought struck her. This wouldn't be a ruse, a way to get her to talk to him because she'd ignored his gifts and messages?

No, of course not. Max had integrity. He wouldn't lie to get sympathy. Besides, she'd recognised the slightly panicky note in his voice. She'd heard it before when a client had had problems with a computer system—they knew how to use the system but not how to fix the problems if it crashed.

Which was where she came in. Today, she'd fix Max's computer, retrieve his files, and then leave. Debt paid. Nothing more to say.

And at least Lisa would be there. She'd be a buffer between them. Max wouldn't make any moves in front of his secretary—Cyn's best friend. Would he?

To Cyn's surprise, Max answered the door himself. He looked stunning, in dark trousers and a dark round-necked sweater; the same as he'd worn the night of the gallery party. The night where he'd kissed her beside the Thames. The night she'd spent here, in his bed. Her heart missed a beat at the memory.

He also looked worried sick and there were shadows under his eyes. She itched to reach out and touch his cheek, smooth away the worry lines. Though she wouldn't. Touching him would be a bad move. Weaken her resolve. She'd fall into bed with him again—and he'd break her heart.

'Hello, Cyn. Thanks for coming,' he said quietly.

'You're welcome.' Her voice *would* have to squeak, wouldn't it? Oh, great. Well, she didn't want him thinking it was his nearness that had that effect on her—even though it was. 'I'm doing this because I owe you for rescuing me at the wedding,' she told him quietly. 'Paying my debt.'

Once she'd fixed his computer, they'd be quits. And she could walk out of his life. For ever.

'You're not in my debt. But if you fix this, I'm sure as hell going to be in yours. Can I get you some coffee before you start?' he asked.

She shook her head. 'No, thanks. Where's Lisa?'

'I sent her out to buy some sandwiches. I thought she'd know what you liked.'

'You didn't have to do that.' In some respects, she wished he hadn't. Or that he'd gone himself, so she'd had time to prepare herself for seeing him again.

Ha. All the time in the world wouldn't have been enough to prepare herself for seeing him again. He still sent her weak at the knees, even though she'd schooled herself all the way here to be cool, calm and collected.

'Where's the machine?' she asked, knowing she sounded abrupt, but not knowing how else to deal with the feelings flooding through her. Once she set to work, she knew she'd be fine, so the quicker she got to his computer, the better. 'Let me have a look at it, and I'll tell you if it's fixable—and how long it's going to take.'

Without further comment, he ushered her into his office. One look at the screen had her sighing. 'Looks like a virus attack. Don't you have virus protection software? Or a firewall?'

'Firewall?' He looked blank.

'You're just plug-and-play, aren't you?' she asked wryly.

'Look, it's just my computer.' He flapped his hands dismissively. 'It's where I store my work.'

'In other words, it's your livelihood. You should protect it better.'

'I've got a virus checker,' he protested.

'Is it up to date?'

'It does everything automatically.'

And it was obvious he didn't have a clue how it worked. Wouldn't know if it had gone wrong. 'You're a business, Max. You connect to the net and that leaves your machine wide open for attack. You really need a firewall as well. Do you keep a backup of your files on Lisa's machine?'

He winced. 'Er, no. I do keep backups, though. On a CD-ROM,' he offered.

'A flash drive is more reliable,' she said. 'As long as you back up regularly. And by that I mean do it every single night—it takes less than ten minutes to transfer all your files, and literally seconds to copy the latest versions of your files. It also means you'll never lose more than a single day's work if something goes wrong. Do the backups on CD once a week, too.'

'You do this often, don't you?' Max asked, sounding rueful.

'Yup. And it's usually a repeat job for a client who's been caught once and promised they'll never, ever do it again. As time passes, so does the memory of how scared they were when they thought they'd lost everything. Then they get complacent. Forget to do their backups. They panic, the first time, but then they discover they got away with it and they really let it slide—that extra five minutes a day gets eaten up. Before they know it, it's a couple of months since they did their last backup. And, bam, they get caught again—and they're left in a mess.' She shrugged. 'Right. The first thing we need to do is get you working again. Do you use the same software on Lisa's machine as you do on yours?'

He shook his head. 'Not all of it. I do my notes in the same word-processing program she uses, but the design software is just on mine.'

'Do you have the master disks for your software?'

He looked fidgety. 'Somewhere, yes.' He raked a hand through his hair. 'I leave the admin to Lisa. She'll know where they are.'

'Good. If you can find them, and your last backup, we'll do a quick temporary fix—we'll install the software on my laptop.'

'On your laptop?' he queried, sounding surprised.

'First rule of troubleshooting. Get the client back to normal as quickly as possible. Time's money, in business—and I won't be using my laptop while I'm fixing your machine. So I'll set you up on my laptop and you can at least keep working while I sort out the problems.'

'Thank you.'

Though, as Cyn had suspected, when Lisa came back and found the software master disks for her, it turned out that Max's backup routines were haphazard. The last disk he'd used was corrupted, and the one before that was dated from months before, so it didn't have the files he wanted on it.

'He's been nobbled,' Lisa said, looking furious.

'You don't know that for sure. Magnetic media isn't perfect—disks corrupt all the time, even CD-ROMs,' Cyn said.

'But you can physically corrupt a disk?' Lisa persisted.

Cyn nodded. 'It's possible, yes. But you're being paranoid, Lise. Joe's obviously got you to prompt him on too many conspiracy theory scripts.' She turned to Max. 'Looks as if I'll have to do this the long way. But, as I said, feel free to use my laptop until I've fixed your machine. You can at least work on some of your current stuff.'

'You are going to be able to get my stuff back?' he asked.

She bit her lip. 'I can't promise I can retrieve all your data. It depends on which sort of virus hit you—whether it's a worm, a Trojan or another sort of virus. Different ones screw up different types of files.'

He pulled a face. 'You're talking a different language.'

'Techie speak,' Lisa said. 'Tell me about it. She does it all the time at home.'

'Just ignore me,' Cyn said. 'I'll be as quick as I can.'

'I'll try not to get in your way,' Max said.

A tall order, considering how aware of him Cyn was. Her body remembered his touch and wanted more. Wanted to press itself up against him and feel the heat of his skin. Feel the strength of his muscles tensing as he lowered himself onto her. Feel his body becoming part of hers.

Well, tough. It wasn't going to happen, so she'd just have to exercise a bit of will power.

Then she noticed that, although Lisa had left her to it, Max had lingered.

'What?' she asked.

'You take your coffee black, don't you?' he asked.

He remembered? She damped down the surge of pleasure. 'Techie safety rules, number one. Never trust the milk.'

'Why?'

She smiled. 'Because most techies never quite got out of the student lifestyle. You get involved in programming and you don't think about anything else—and even if you remember to check the sell-by date on the milk, there's no guarantee that you know what day it is anyway. So either you get into the habit of sniffing the milk first, or…'

'I get the picture,' he said with a grimace. 'Black coffee coming up.'

He didn't interrupt her as such, when he walked back into the room, though her body was screaming, 'He's here! He's here!' Cyn sipped the coffee absently, trying to concentrate on the task before her.

She soon had her laptop in working order for him, and set it up on the table next to his drawing-board. A little while later, she found out what the problem was with his machine, and sucked her teeth.

'What is it?' Max asked immediately. Almost as if he'd been watching her, waiting for her to do or say something. Though that was silly. Of course he hadn't.

'Your problem is something that's called a Trojan horse—it's called that because the file contains a hidden program, pretty much like the Greeks hiding inside the wooden horse they sent to Troy,' she explained.

'So what does this Trojan thing do?' he asked, coming to stand beside her.

'Depends on the program. Most of the time, it means your computer's sending your passwords or other data to someone else's computer.'

'So it was deliberately aimed at me?' He stared at her, shocked.

'Not necessarily—but it's a possibility, yes.'

'What's the bottom line?'

'I have to back up your hard disk, reformat it, reinstall the operating system and your applications, check all your data files, then reinstall them when I'm sure they're clean.'

'You're going to wipe my computer?' he asked.

She nodded.

His face whitened. 'Could I lose what's left of my data? I mean, for good?'

She had to be honest with him. 'It's a possibility, yes.'

'Do you have to wipe it?'

'It's the only way to get your machine clean again.'

He blew out a breath. 'I could lose my data.' Said slowly. As if it was too scary to believe.

'Or it could have been transferred out of your machine already. I might be able to find a hidden copy somewhere, but…' She shrugged. 'Let's just hope you've been lucky.'

'Someone can do that? Someone could steal my files from another computer?'

'Yes.'

He blinked hard, as if trying to get his head round the idea. 'Can you stop it?'

'I can fix it,' she said.

He nodded. 'Then do it. Please.' He swallowed. 'And if my files are gone, can you find out where they went?'

She raised an eyebrow. 'You're asking me to hack into someone else's computer?'

Clearly he hadn't realised the implications of his request, because his eyes widened. 'Oh. I imagine that's illegal?'

'Yes. Though my view is that if someone hacks you, they're fair game for being hacked back,' she said softly. 'What I'm doing is really computer forensics—tracing everything back. Even if they're extremely clever, whoever did this will have left footprints.'

'Footprints?' he echoed, sounding mystified.

'You walk on a solid surface, you leave footprints. You do something in cyberspace, and you leave some sort of signals behind—a kind of electronic pathway. Footprints.'

'And you can follow these footprints?'

She nodded. 'They could have bounced the data anywhere round the world—that is, put out a false trail—but, given time, I can trace it through to the end and track them down.' She raked a hand through her hair. 'What would be helpful is knowing if anyone bears you a grudge—or if you've done anything to upset anyone, recently?'

The air almost hummed with tension. 'Apart from you, you mean?' Max asked.

Her eyes widened in shock. She was a computer whiz. His computer was in ruins. Had he *really* made a connection that wasn't there? Did he honestly think she'd do something like that, because he hadn't called her? Her chin lifted. 'If you think *I* planned this…'

'No. *No!*' he said hastily. 'I didn't mean it to come out like that. What I meant was, I can't think of anyone I've upset. I've made a mess of things with you, and I'm sorry for that. I wanted to see you again, yes—but not in these circumstances. And you wouldn't do anything like this to me anyway.'

'How do you know?' she asked.

'Because I'm a good judge of character. And you have integrity.'

'I have the skills to do it.'

'But you still wouldn't do it,' he insisted. 'You're not a back-door operator. You wouldn't hurt someone by stealth. You'd face a problem head-on—just like you did with the wedding.'

'When I took a trophy boyfriend along and faked it, you mean?'

'I don't remember any faking,' he said softly. 'You were there with me.'

The air thrummed between them. Yes, she'd been there with him. Danced with him. Kissed him. Slept in his arms. Made love with him.

All her limbs seemed to have turned to lead. And her brain was definitely resembling cotton wool. Time to get some professional distance in there. She looked away. 'I'm trying to fix your system, here. Let's concentrate on that, shall we?'

'Sure. I'll go back to my drawing-board and let you get on. But in answer to your question, no, I can't think of anyone I've upset.'

'So this guy who's claiming you stole his ideas…you haven't had a run-in with him?'

'I've never even heard of him before today,' Max said quietly. 'I know the firm, Rutter's—it's a fairly large one, but not one I've had dealings with. It's not my old firm. I can't think of anything other than the normal business rivalry,' he said. 'And this definitely isn't normal. You just don't *do* this to a business rival. You let your designs speak for themselves. It's the client's choice, at the end of the day.'

'Have you had any other business problems recently? Something that might be linked?' Cyn asked.

He frowned. 'Yeah. I've lost a few tenders, lately. People who've changed their mind and gone with someone else. I did wonder this morning if it might be linked with this.'

'Could be.' She nodded. 'Who did they go with? The same firm as the one that's saying you copied their designs?'

'I don't think so. I haven't been able to pin anything down.'

'Right. Well, I'll start digging. It might take me a couple of days,' she warned.

Days? He was having trouble concentrating when she'd only been around for an hour or so. And he was definitely having trouble keeping his hands to himself. Every time he looked up and saw her concentrating on the screen, he wanted to walk over to her desk—*his* desk—grab her, and kiss her. Weird. Even in that anonymous grey business suit, she was the most desirable woman he'd ever met. Particularly as he remembered what she looked like underneath that suit. What she felt like. God, he wanted to touch her! Touch her and taste her and lose himself in her and forget this nightmare. 'Days?' he croaked.

She shrugged. 'If you'd kept proper backups, it wouldn't be a problem, would it?'

She was seriously scary, in business mode. Cool, efficient, a little bit abrupt. The best at what she did—he knew at a gut level that if anyone could fix this, she could. But her eyes were cool when she looked at him, not warm with desire as they had been last Friday night. Friday, when she'd come apart in his arms and he'd seen it in her eyes.

Today, she'd made it very clear she wasn't interested. If he pushed her now, she'd walk out of his life. Which would leave his business *and* his personal life in rubble. He had to back off. Now. Regroup. 'Point taken.'

She took out her mobile phone. 'I'll ring the office and let them know I'll be out for a while—that I definitely won't be back today and maybe not on Monday, either.'

'You're taking holiday to do this? But—no, that's not fair. You said this is going to take a while, and I don't expect you to give up your time for nothing.' He frowned. 'I'll pay you a consultancy fee. Invoice me for whatever the going rate is and I'll see Lisa pays you by bank transfer, the same day.'

She shook her head. 'Firstly, it's time in lieu—they owe me some. A lot, actually. Secondly, as I said, it's payback from me to you, for the wedding. You wouldn't let me pay for the room—or even my half.'

The room. Oh, Lord, that hotel room. When she'd dropped the towel and he'd seen her curves in the mirror... When he'd woken to find her stroking his body... When he'd explored her body extremely thoroughly with his hands and his mouth, and taken her over the edge of pleasure...

He definitely couldn't stand up for the next five minutes or so, or she'd notice exactly what his problem was. And he'd better start running through some mathematics in his head, to get his mind off thoughts of Cyn's naked body. More particularly, to stop himself thinking of how close his bed was, and how easy it would be to carry her upstairs. Just as he'd carried her there last week. Before peeling off her clothes and making long, slow love with her. All night.

'Is she doing what I think she's doing?' Lisa asked Max in a stage whisper, standing a mug of coffee on each of their desks.

'If you mean did I call the office and say I'm taking time off, yes,' Cyn said coolly as she cut the connection on her phone. 'Time in lieu.'

Lisa scoffed. 'You *never* take time in lieu.'

'I do now.' A muscle flickered in her jaw.

Lisa frowned. 'What's happened?'

'Nothing.'

The denial was too fast, and Cyn clearly knew it, because Max noticed that she didn't meet his eyes—or Lisa's.

'You were meant to hear about the promotion today. Are they making you wait until Monday, now?' Lisa asked.

'No. They've sent the letters out.'

'Hang on. Are you saying you didn't get the promotion?' Lisa asked in shock.

'Bull's-eye,' Cyn said.

Cyn had gone for promotion and hadn't got it? 'Why?' Max asked.

'Apparently, I put too many hours in. I don't have a rounded social profile.' Cyn shrugged. 'So I'm working office hours, from now on. And I'm taking the time in lieu that's owed to me. If there's a problem, Rob or Gus from my team will text me.'

'But—that's ridiculous. Of course you have a rounded social profile. You go out, don't you? And it's not a good enough reason for not giving you the promotion,' Max said. 'If you're the best at what you do and you work hard, you deserve the job.'

'That's not how our human resources department sees it,' Cyn said tightly.

'What are you going to do?' Lisa asked.

'For the moment, I'll stay at RCS. But I'm thinking seriously about finding another job. Maybe I'll go freelance, work for myself. I've got a decent reputation.'

Just what Max had thought about himself. Except now he'd crashed and burned. And he'd realised now just how fragile reputations could be. 'It's a risk,' he warned.

'One that's going to be worth taking.'

Yeah, but it wasn't the risk he wanted her to take. He wanted her to take the risk with him. And somehow he had to find a way of telling her, without scaring her off for good.

By the end of the office day, Cyn was still working on the data.

'I'm going home now,' Lisa said from the doorway.

'Um, if you want to leave now, Cyn...?' Max asked.

She shook her head. 'I'm just starting to really get some-where. I'll carry on for a bit longer, if you don't mind.'

'She loves doing forensic stuff. You'll have to throw her out,' Lisa predicted. 'Or maybe I should ring you both at ten to tell you to get your butts out of the office.'

'There's no need. I won't make Cyn slave that late at night,' Max protested.

'You won't have to. She'll do that all by herself,' Lisa said wryly. 'And you're just as bad.'

'I'll send her home before eight,' Max promised.

'A likely story. See you when I see you, Cyn. And unless you need me in tomorrow—in which case, just text me—I'll see you on Monday, boss,' Lisa said, closing the door behind her.

So there they were. Just the two of them. Too close for comfort, Cyn thought. But Max had kept his distance during the day. He'd continue to do it during the evening, too. She hoped—because it was stupid to hope for what she really wanted.

That he would do the opposite.

That he'd touch her again.

That he'd sweep her off her feet and kiss all her doubts away.

At half past seven, Max switched off the light over his drawing board. 'What would you like for dinner?'

He was planning to take her out to dinner? 'No need,' she said stiffly. 'I'll get a take-away delivered when I get home.'

'You've been working flat out all day. You haven't had a break—and I'm starving, so you must be too.'

Well, yes. She was hungry.

'It won't take me long to knock something together—and it's as easy to cook for two as it is for one.'

He was going to cook for her? The men of Cyn's ac-quaintance weren't domesticated. The nearest they came to preparing a meal was phoning for a take-away. They certainly wouldn't know how to make a meal from scratch.

And then she remembered the email he'd sent her.

I love cooking—and I'm *good* at things I love doing.

Oh, dear.

At least he didn't comment on her silence. 'Thai okay with you?' he asked.

'Fine.' More than fine. She adored Thai food.

'Twenty minutes, then. My kitchen's at the top of the stairs, turn left.' He grinned. 'Follow your nose.'

She didn't last for twenty minutes. The scent was just too good. Lemon grass, coconut milk, ginger—she recognised the smells. And they made her even hungrier. When she reached the kitchen doorway, she stood there, just watching him. Max was a methodical cook, efficient and neat; from the look of it, he'd chopped everything and put it neatly into bowls ready to be scraped into the pan, then stacked the bowls up as he emptied them.

And the look on his face: concentrated, intense. Just like the way he worked at his draughtboard.

Just like the way he made love.

With an effort, she pushed the idea out of her mind, and walked into the kitchen. 'Hi.'

'Hi.'

'Your kitchen's amazing.'

'Thank you.'

Last time she'd been at his place, she hadn't got the chance to see it. Because he'd carried her up two flights of stairs straight to his bed, at the top of the house. They'd taken a rain check on the tour of the rest of the building. Oh, hell. That was definitely something she shouldn't be thinking about. She needed to focus on the room, not on memories of sex with Max.

He'd installed a traditional Shaker kitchen in light oak, adding granite worktops and top-notch appliances. Dream kitchen. But this wasn't a show kitchen; it was definitely a cook's kitchen. Max was perfectly at ease there. For a second, she could imagine working with him in that kitchen: making things together, popping teasing morsels in each other's mouths, getting distracted by each other...

Whoa. She'd promised herself she wouldn't go there.

'I love my house,' he said softly.

She could hear the fear in his voice: that he'd lose everything he'd worked for. He'd told her how he'd fallen in love with a pile of rubble, mortgaged himself to the hilt and roughed it until he could afford to do it up the way he'd seen it in his head.

And it was in her power now to make sure he didn't lose it. 'Don't worry, Max. I'll find out the truth. I'll prove that those designs are yours and clear your name.'

His face said the words he clearly didn't want to utter: *I hope so.* 'Thank you. If you want to make yourself useful, you can lay the table. The cutlery's in there.' He nodded towards a drawer.

Glad of something to do, she laid the table. A couple of minutes later, he dished up sticky coconut rice and Thai chicken.

'It's very good,' she said after her first mouthful.

'Thank you.'

Though it was hardly surprising that Max was a good cook. His claim hadn't been empty. He was extremely good at things he liked doing. Her stomach clenched as she remembered the feel of his hands on her skin, his mouth against hers. Teasing. Tempting. Inciting her to go wild.

When would this longing go away?

She didn't trust herself to speak. Her awkwardness must have transmitted itself to Max because he didn't speak either.

Crazy. Considering they'd talked and talked, the night they'd walked down the Thames together. About buildings and music and poetry—

No. Not a good idea to think about poetry. Or the lines he'd quoted at her.

'Before, behind, between, above, below.'

What he'd done with her.

Because she wasn't going to let it happen again. She wasn't going to lose her heart to Max and watch him walk out of her life when he panicked. Max and commitment just didn't go together. She had to remember that.

She refused his offer of pudding and coffee. And he refused her offer of helping with the washing up.

'I'll drive you home,' Max said, taking his keys out of his pocket. 'My car's fixed now.'

'No need. I can get the tube.'

'Cyn, it's late. And it's the least I can do, considering you're about to save my neck.'

Neck? Yeah—hers was stiff. She shuffled surreptitiously, hoping to ease the ache, but he noticed.

'You spent too long sitting in one position.'

Yes, well. It was her own fault. She knew better than to sit hunched over a keyboard without a break. The health and safety people at RCS were forever giving training sessions on how to avoid RSI. Though the techies were all guilty of ignoring the advice when they were involved in a project. They got caught up in what they were doing and, without a timer to remind them, they didn't think to take proper breaks. And she was definitely guilty of grabbing a sandwich at her desk and working through her lunch hour, most days. 'I'm fine,' she fibbed.

'No, you're not.' He slid his keys back into his pocket and walked behind her. 'Sit. Don't argue.'

To her mingled horror and pleasure, he began to massage her neck and shoulders. His touch was firm and sure, and within a couple of minutes he'd eased the kinks out of her muscles.

It felt so good. She closed her eyes, leaning forward slightly. So good. And supposing he lowered his head now, followed the movement of his fingers with his mouth? Just as he had that night in the hotel, when he'd kissed the back of her neck and sent desire surging through her. Just as he had when he'd kissed her all over in his big, wide bed.

She clung to the remnants of her common sense. This had to stop. Right now. 'Thank you. I'm fine now.' And please take your hands off me before I do something stupid, she added silently. Like begging you to carry me to your bed again.

What would it be like to live with someone who could do this for you? The man of her dreams. Intelligent, sexy, and so very skilled with his hands. In so many ways.

She shook herself. Stupid. She wasn't even going out with him, let alone planning to live with him. Think of all the times you've seen your mum crying, she told herself. Max didn't even ring you when he said he would—how can you trust him with more? Do you want to end up like your mum, breaking your heart over yet another man who's let you down?

'I'll take you home,' Max said quietly.

She collected her handbag from his office. 'I'll leave the laptop with you for now. I'm not planning to do any more work tonight, and it'll save me hauling it around on the tube tomorrow morning.'

'I can pick you up tomorrow, if you want?' he offered.

'No, I'll be fine.'

'It wouldn't be a problem. And the offer's open, so call me if you change your mind.' He locked the front door and ushered her to his car.

The low-slung two-seater: when she'd last sat in it, he'd kissed her for the first time. Thoroughly.

Cyn made sure that she buckled her own seat belt, this time. She didn't trust herself. The lightest brush of her skin against his, and she'd be tempted to grab him. Best to avoid temptation. She was supposed to be training herself to fall *out* of love with him, not deeper *in* love with him.

It seemed to take hours until he finally pulled up outside her house and switched off the engine.

Kiss me.

The desire was so strong, it was like a physical pain. But the only way to ease it would be to do something that would cause her a great deal more pain in the future. So she was going to play it safe.

She undid her seat belt.

But before she had the chance to climb out of the car, his hand circled her wrist. 'Cyn.'

She turned to look at him. Mistake. Big mistake. Those gorgeous blue eyes had her melting in seconds.

'Thank you for coming to my rescue.' He raised her hand to his mouth and kissed each knuckle in turn.

'No worries,' she croaked.

His lips were still grazing her skin. Sensitising it. Since when had the back of her hand been an erogenous zone?

His gaze was fixed intently on hers as he turned her hand over, pressed a kiss into her palm and folded her fingers over it. 'Cyn. We've still got unfinished business.'

'No, we haven't.' She pulled her hand back. 'And I can't…if you push me…'

'I don't want to push you,' he whispered, 'but it's there. That spark between us. I've never felt—'

'Stop. Please. I can't do this.' Well, she could. But she wanted to keep her heart in one piece. Which it wouldn't be, if she let Max make love to her. Because tonight would be the third time.

The *last* time.

Better to leave it now and keep her heart intact. 'I'll see you tomorrow,' she said, climbing out of the car. And she closed the door without waiting for his reply.

CHAPTER FIFTEEN

THE house seemed empty when Max returned. Which was crazy. He loved his house. He'd always felt comfortable in it, even when it had been more or less a pile of rubble inside and had had no heating whatsoever. It had always been enough for him. His dream.

But he'd shared his office today—something he hadn't done since going solo. He liked his own space, which was why he'd given Lisa an office of her own. And yet it had felt good today, working with Cyn across the other side of the room from him. Okay, so he hadn't been at his most productive—every so often, he'd looked up from his desk and just watched her working. That intense, focused look on her face—she'd had that same look when they'd made love. His body tightened as he remembered carrying Cyn to his bed. Remembered pushing deep, deep inside her. Remembered the feel of her body tightening round his.

He swallowed hard. Hell. Tonight, it would have been so easy to start it all over again. That stupid impulse to massage her neck… Luckily she'd been the one to call a halt. If she hadn't, he knew where she'd have ended up, and it wouldn't have been her own bed. And the only thing she'd have been wearing was *him*.

He groaned. He needed to feel Cyn's body wrapped round his again. It wasn't just lust. It was something more than that—something that made him want to run as fast as he could in the opposite direction from her. Yet, at the same time, he wanted to run straight to her.

Ah, hell. He knew this feeling. The same feeling he'd had when he'd first seen his house. He'd known there were going to be huge challenges, but he'd fallen in love with it at first sight.

His house.

His woman.

Same feeling. Which meant this was the real thing. She was The One.

Oh, Lord. He was in love with Cyn Reynolds. In love with a woman who right now was as wary of him as an alley cat. And with good reason, because his past was everything she didn't want. Mr No-Commitment.

Somehow, he was going to have to persuade her to give him another chance. To give them a chance. To make her realise that, with her, he was different—that he could do commitment where she was concerned.

Saturday was much like Friday. Cyn said a polite hello to Max; and then was instantly absorbed in her work. Max brought her a mug of coffee, without comment; she murmured thanks but barely seemed to notice him.

Whereas Max couldn't take his eyes off her. He was talking on the phone and realised that he'd completely missed what his client had just said, because he'd been too busy watching the copper glints in Cyn's hair, or noticing the way her fingers flew across the keyboard, or the way she caught the tip of her tongue between her teeth when she was concentrating.

He turned away to concentrate on his call.

He'd just put the phone down when he heard a quiet but intense, 'Yes!' and the whirr of his printer.

He looked over to see her smiling broadly. 'Have you found something?' he asked.

'Your computer is now unglued. Your files are all still there—and they're date-stamped. I'm just printing off the stats.'

'Stats?'

'Your word-processing files have a section which shows when the file was first created, how many revisions you've made, how long you spent working on it and when you last accessed it,' she explained.

It was news to him. And he obviously looked blank because she grinned. 'Before you ask, yes, it can be altered—by someone who knows what they're doing. But that means messing about with a computer's clock, and any techie would know within three seconds of talking to you that you wouldn't have a clue how to do it. I'd say you're in the clear.'

'I…I dunno what to say. Just that you're brilliant.' And I want to kiss you.

His mouth went dry. God, he wanted to kiss her. Wrap his arms round her. Feel her wrapped round him.

'I owe you,' he said huskily.

'No, this is payback for the way you stopped the gossip at Michelle Wilson's wedding. And I haven't finished, yet. I'm going to track down whoever did it. Now, has anyone except Lisa had access to your computer?'

'No.' He frowned. 'Well, maybe. I did a favour for a friend and had someone with me on work experience for a while, about a year back. Charlotte. Apparently she wanted to be an architect but her family wouldn't take her seriously.' Something that had pressed all his buttons. Brought all his guilt tumbling back to the surface. 'She was taking a year out before starting university and thought if she got some work experience it would help her cause.' His client and old friend Alice had asked him to help Charlotte, as a favour to her. So of course he'd said yes.

'And this work experience took place while you were working on these files? Or with any of the clients you lost?' Cyn queried.

'Yes. The first one, actually—Phil Watkins.' He explained about the magazine article and how it had aroused his suspicions.

Cyn nodded. 'So she could have taken your designs.'

He frowned. 'Charlotte? No way. She'd only be partway through her first year of an architecture degree—she wouldn't have been able to pass herself off as qualified, and she certainly wouldn't be able to say the designs were her own. She couldn't have said it was a student project, because there was stuff she wouldn't have learned about yet on those designs. Besides, she was just a kid. Eighteen.'

'Age doesn't have anything to do with it,' Cyn said dryly. 'Hackers tend to start young.'

He shook his head. 'She couldn't have done it, Cyn. Really. She was shadowing me, learning all about what the job really entails, so she was with me all the time.'

'Including when you were in meetings?'

'Yes.'

'All of them?'

'Most of them. Except the ones where the client requested confidentiality,' he admitted. 'The ones where she wasn't with me, she was helping Lisa with filing and stuff.'

'And if Lisa was busy, she wouldn't have overseen every single bit of filing. So Charlotte did have the opportunity, both to fiddle with your computer and to remove your paper files.'

'Well, yes, I suppose so,' he admitted. 'But she didn't have a motive.'

'Hmm,' was all Cyn said.

'You think she did it?'

'Maybe. But you're right, she couldn't pass herself off as a qualified architect. Which means she has to be working with someone who is. My guess is it's the guy who claimed you stole his design. So we need to find a link between them.' Cyn frowned. 'Trust me on this. I'm going to have a word with the Oracle.'

'The Oracle?' Max echoed.

'Lise. That's what we called her at RCS, because she knows everything and everyone. If my theory's right, she'll get us the proof.'

'Hang on. You can't just accuse people—'

'Without proof,' Cyn cut in. 'Which is why I'm going to ask Lisa to check a few things out for me.'

'Anything I can do?'

'Just sit tight,' she said. 'I'll handle this.'

He was about to protest; then he saw the look in her eyes. Payback, she'd said. For once, she was the one doing the rescuing instead of the one being rescued. This would make things even between them, in her view.

And then, maybe, they'd have the chance to start again. A clean slate. No rescuing on either side. Equals.

Yeah. He could do that. He'd wait. Because she was worth it.

Lisa arrived mid-afternoon, made a few phone calls, then walked into Max's office with a tray of coffee and chocolate biscuits. 'You're going to need this,' she warned.

'Do I need to call my solicitor?' Max asked.

Lisa nodded. 'It's not good. You know how you drag me off to these architectural dos from time to time—well, I know a few of the other secretaries fairly well now. I had a chat to…' She paused. 'Well, her name isn't important.

I promised I'd keep her out of it. But Jason Henry's name is definitely important.'

'Who's Jason Henry?' Cyn asked.

'The architect who claims I stole his designs. He's a rising star at Rutter's, one of the biggest practices in the city,' Max explained.

'Not that much of a star,' Lisa said. 'Apparently, he hasn't been living up to his early promise. His position at Rutter's is a bit wobbly, to say the least. He's brought in a couple of good clients over the last year, but not enough to please his boss. He's made some careless mistakes—mistakes that were easy to fix but cost the firm money. And it seems that winning the competition—getting column inches for positive reasons and proving he's got what it takes in design terms—is about his only hope of keeping his job. So he needed a sure-fire winning entry. And our Max's design was the best bet.'

'Jason Henry's an architect, not a techie. And he doesn't even *know* me—at least, I can't ever remember meeting him. So how the hell could he have accessed my designs?' Max shook his head. 'It doesn't stack up, Lise.'

'I'm afraid it does. Because Jason Henry,' Lisa told him quietly, 'has a girlfriend. She's a bit younger than he is. Nineteen years old. Name of Helen Jones.'

Max drummed his fingers on his desk. 'So that puts Charlotte in the clear, then.'

'Unfortunately not,' Lisa said. 'I described her to my contact—who told me that she sounded exactly like Jason's girlfriend. Helen Jones changes her hair colour every three weeks, but apart from that she's the same height, has the same eye colour, and even dresses the same as Charlotte. So it has to be her.'

Max shook his head. 'It can't be. There must be some kind of mistake. Coincidence. Charlotte's a friend of a friend of Alice's. Alice is an old friend of mine—she gave me my first break when I went solo,' he explained to Cyn. 'I've restored a couple of places for her now.'

'It looks as if Helen conned Alice as well. Appealed to her motherly instincts,' Lisa said with a sigh. 'Max, I hate to be the one to tell you this, but Helen Jones's middle name is Charlotte. It's not a coincidence.'

Max raked a hand through his hair. 'I…I can't take this in.'

'Sorry, Max. I think we've found our thief. The thing is, Helen doesn't want to be an architect at all. She's a techie. She's taking a gap year before going to Manchester to do a degree in computing,' Lisa said.

'I told you, hackers start young,' Cyn said dryly. 'If she's that bright, all she had to do was hack into the competition files, find out who her boyfriend was up against, work out which one was most likely to win, and target that person.'

'Me?' Max frowned.

'You're the obvious target. I did an Internet search on you myself. It brought up page after page about the rising star of the architectural world, Max Taylor. You were tipped to win the competition. Some of them even called you "King Max".'

'Oh, that's *too* much,' he protested, pulling a face. 'I'm an architect, that's all!'

'But you're a star in your world.' Cyn shrugged. 'So you were the obvious choice. And she spun you a sob story that was guaranteed to press your buttons.'

He came to sit on the edge of Cyn's desk. 'There's no way she could have known about that.'

'It might have been in one of the profiles on the Net. Or maybe she talked to some people who knew you. She's young; she's attractive. At a party, she could have flirted with someone who thought he'd never get a smile from a pretty girl, and charmed him into telling her all about you—and he wouldn't have had the faintest idea that she was pumping him for information, because he'd been so bowled over at the fact she was paying him attention,' Cyn suggested. 'Or maybe she'd confessed to a particularly motherly secretary that she had this terrible crush on you; and the secretary wanted to protect her from someone who wouldn't date her more than three times before dumping her and refusing to return her calls.'

'Oh, come on.' Max scowled. 'I'm not that bad.'

'Yes, you are,' Lisa said.

'Enough for an older woman to want to look out for a young, innocent girl who had a crush on you and would get her heart broken,' Cyn said.

Oh, Lord. Did Cyn mean herself? That she thought he'd break *her* heart?

'She's right,' Lisa chipped in. 'You've got a reputation. And Helen's a good actress. She conned you. She conned me too—I can usually tell actors a mile off!'

'And when the older woman had finished trying to head Helen off, she'd have felt guilty that she'd been a bit unkind to you. So then she'd have told Helen a bit about you, why you were so driven,' Cyn said. 'It's not hard to work out. You've got a guilt streak a mile long about the fact you should've been a doctor like your dad, so you want to prove you're the best and you don't have time for relationships.'

'So all Helen had to do was come and see you, claim she wanted to be an architect and her family was against it, and you'd be there to champion her and offer her some work experience,' Lisa finished.

He groaned. 'I'm that much of a sucker.'

'No. You're known for dating a lot, but businesswise you're known for being fair—you'll give people a chance.

Which was why Alice sent her to you in the first place. Helen would have known that Alice would contact you, because Alice has sung your praises in enough articles in the press. If it hadn't worked with Alice, she'd have tried some of your other old clients, until she found someone who'd put in a good word with you,' Lisa said. 'Just look at your PR cuttings file. She'd have had plenty to choose from.'

'And if she loved Jason that much, she'd do her best to help him win that competition and keep his job—by fair means or foul,' Cyn added. 'In this case, foul. Because she took your files. Being a techie, she knew how to transfer your files without you knowing it.'

'But she left before I even entered the designs,' Max protested. 'The timing was wrong.'

'That's why she left the Trojan behind—so she could still have access to your computer, in case you made any changes to the competition design at the last minute,' Cyn explained. 'And that back-door access meant she could filch a couple of other clients for Jason and buy him a breathing space, when things got a bit rocky at his firm. I bet if you dig deep enough you'll see his name there. It also meant she was able to turn your computer to soup yesterday, when she knew that letter would hit your desk.' She shrugged. 'The odds were that your machine wouldn't be fixed in time for you to get your files back and clear your name. So Jason Henry would've produced his files, which—after some clever work by Helen with the computer clock—were date-stamped to show he'd done the designs months ago. He'd have won the competition with your design, and with the backing of a big company that had no idea how you'd been cheated.'

'So she had the motive and the opportunity,' Max said grimly.

'Exactly,' Cyn said. 'Now all I have to do is find the bit that links the Trojan to her. Now, she's clever, so she wouldn't have done it from her own machine—it'd be too easy to trace back. So she'd probably have used a public access terminal; an Internet café, or something like that. What I need to do now is find out where it was. Once I've found it, we can ask to see their records of who booked their machines and when.'

'They have records like that?' Max asked.

Cyn nodded in confirmation.

'And Helen's a pretty girl. They'll definitely remember her,' Lisa added.

'Max, can you sketch her?' Cyn asked.

'Sketch?' he asked, surprised.

'You're an architect. Which means you can draw, doesn't it?'

He frowned. 'I'm not an artist. I don't usually draw people.'

'But you can do a reasonable likeness?'

'Yes. Then what?'

'I'll scan it in to your computer—you do *have* a scanner, I presume?'

He nodded.

'Good. Then I'll email the picture over to whoever controls the public access terminal she used, and they'll be able to confirm if it was her. Then we can see when she last used the terminal. If the time's the same as the one where your machine was accessed externally, she's caught. And it'll stand up in a court of law,' Cyn said.

It all sounded too good to be true. There had to be a catch. 'Supposing for some reason they don't keep records?'

'They have to,' Cyn said. 'They need to cover their backs, in case someone uses their machines to unleash a virus or hack into a restricted site. Techno-crime is on the up, and the law's going to get tough on it. Public Net access providers would be wise to get their houses in order before they're forced to do it legally.'

'So you're saying that Charlotte—' Max couldn't quite get his head around the idea of calling her Helen '—could get into serious trouble?'

Cyn sighed. 'Don't be sentimental about it, Max. The thing is, if she's done it once and got away with it, she could be tempted to do it again. And the next person might not be so lucky—they might not be able to fix things in time.'

'She's a kid. She doesn't need locking up. She needs help,' Max said.

'Do you want your name cleared, or not?' Lisa asked.

'Yes.' But he remembered the earnest look on Charlotte's face when she'd asked him for some work experience. She'd seemed so interested, so keen. Just as he'd been, at that age.

He'd been suckered. A naïve, stupid fool.

'Hey. We all make mistakes,' Cyn said softly, as if guessing what was going through his head. She closed her hand over his and squeezed, just for a second. 'Don't beat yourself up about it.'

We all make mistakes. Did she mean about Charlotte? Or was she talking about them?

Her eyes gave nothing away. But the warmth of her hand lingered on his skin as he went back to his desk and sketched the girl he'd known as Charlotte.

'I would stay,' Lisa said, an hour or so later, 'but I'm supposed to be going to the opening of a new play, tonight. And I promised Sally I'd be there to support her.'

'There isn't anything else you can do here, to be honest. And I shouldn't be that much longer anyway. I've gone via Australia, America, and half a dozen Eastern European countries,' Cyn said. 'I'm pretty sure I'm going to get back to the source shortly. So go and enjoy your play. Say hi to Sally for me.'

'Sure. I'll ring you in the interval for an update. Or text me, if I don't get a chance to ring you,' Lisa said. She gave her best friend a hug. 'Good luck. Well, not that you need it—you're good at what you do. See you later, Max.'

'Yeah. And thanks for all you've done today.'

'You're welcome.' She grinned. 'Though if you *really* want to make me feel good about putting in some extra time without being paid for it, there's a pair of shoes in the shop round the corner with my name on it…'

'Subtle. Not,' Max said, grinning back. 'It's a deal, Lise. The least I can do.'

Half an hour later, Cyn leaned back in her chair. 'Bingo.'

'You've found the source?'

She nodded. 'London. Just as I thought, our hacker used a café chain.' She raised an eyebrow. 'Give me ten minutes and I'll have proof.'

Max watched her, his heart in his mouth. Her fingers flew across the keyboard as she looked up something on the Internet. A quick phone call and two emails later, her mobile phone rang.

'Cyn Reynolds. Yes. Yes. Uh-huh. Thank you very much. Yes, please do.' She cut the connection. 'Want the good news or the bad?' she asked Max.

'Start with the bad.'

'Lisa was right. It was Helen Jones.' She shrugged. 'So you'd better ring your solicitor.'

'And the good?'

'They have the information we need. You're in the clear.'

He nodded soberly. 'So why do I feel so bad about it?'

'Because you're a nice guy.'

He closed his eyes briefly. 'This is a mess. If I put this in the hands of my lawyers, Jason's career is over and Charlotte—I mean Helen—will be kicked out of college.'

'If you don't, they'll think they've got away with it and they'll do it again,' Cyn warned. 'Anyway, Jason's career isn't necessarily over. It's his first serious mistake. A stupid mistake. He was desperate—he panicked and lost his way. Someone will give him a chance to make up for it. And Helen needs to be stopped before she lands herself in really serious trouble.'

'Yeah.' He rubbed his hand across his eyes. 'I suppose.'

'Just ring your lawyer,' she said quietly. 'The main thing is to clear your name. We can work something out afterwards.'

By the time he'd finished the call, she'd packed up her laptop and her disks. His eyes widened. 'You're going?'

'I've done my job,' she said simply. 'And I've sent Lisa a text to tell her what happened, so you don't need to worry about trying to get hold of her.'

'But…' He didn't want Cyn to go. He didn't want her to walk out of his life. He caught her hand. 'Cyn…'

'Yes?'

Her eyes were huge. Fear? Anticipation? Or both? He already knew he'd hurt her. But he'd hurt them both a lot more if he didn't stop her going right now.

'Thank you,' he said, and bent his head.

The second his mouth touched hers, it was as if something had snapped. All the fear, all the misery, just vanished—and there was only Cyn.

Filling his senses completely.

Making him whole.

He wasn't sure when they'd moved from his office. How they'd got upstairs. Or even who'd taken off whose clothes. All he knew was that they were exactly where he wanted them to be. In his bed. Skin to skin. Kissing. Touching. Stroking. Exploring.

Please, God, let this be real. Don't let it be another of those dreams where, when you wake, you cry to dream again.

Her skin was so soft. She smelled so sweet, like strawberries and cream. And he couldn't get enough of her. He loved her responsiveness. He loved the way he could make such a brilliant woman's mind turn to mush. But most of all, he just loved her.

Love.

Commitment.

Shouldn't he be out of this bed in record time and running? But, he realised with shock, he didn't want to move. At all. Because, the more he thought about it, the more it didn't seem such a bad idea. He loved her. He wanted to be with her.

Now, all he had to do was convince her.

'You're so beautiful,' he whispered. 'You make me ache.'

'Max, I—'

He touched one finger gently to her lips, stopping her words. 'Later. We'll talk later, I promise. But for now I need to do what I wanted to do the minute I first saw you. What I've been wanting to do ever since. What I haven't been able to stop thinking about since the night you slept in my arms.' He rubbed his nose against hers, and murmured in her ear, 'I need to be inside you, Cyn.'

CHAPTER SIXTEEN

CYN closed her eyes and tipped her head back against the pillow. 'Yes.'

This time, when Max kissed her, it was different. Because he'd admitted the truth to himself. A truth he wasn't quite ready to admit to her yet—he wanted some time to get used to it himself, first. But he loved her. Mind and body and heart and soul.

He traced the line of her collar-bone with his mouth, and she tipped her head further back, offering him her throat, where her pulse beat hard against its base. Max touched the tip of his tongue to it, feeling it speed up.

This wasn't sex, not the way she reacted to him. It was more than that. Something special. Something he'd never really felt before.

Slowly he moved down, caressing her breasts with his hands and his mouth, taking his time. Revelling in her sweet scent, the velvety smoothness of her skin, the softness of her curves.

'Yes,' she hissed, threading her fingers through his hair. 'Please. Now.'

Oh, no. He wasn't ready yet. He wanted to take this slow and easy. He wanted to fan the flames until they were both at meltdown. He took one nipple into his mouth and sucked hard; she gasped, and he smiled against her skin. He wanted to take Cyn to her limits. And then some.

Slowly, he moved southwards. Circled her navel with the tip of his tongue. Nuzzled the soft swell of her belly.

'Max.' His name came out as a plea. 'Now.'

'Mmm.' He stroked her thighs. 'We have all the time in the world.'

She tilted her hips impatiently, and he rocked back on his haunches. 'Patience is a business asset,' he reminded her.

'This isn't business.'

'No,' he agreed. 'It's pleasure. And there's going to be more. So much more,' he promised.

She quivered, and pushed against him.

He flattened his palms against her thighs and dipped his head. At the first slow stroke of his tongue, Cyn's fingers tightened in his hair. 'Oh, yes. Yes.'

She was hyperventilating when he raised his head and sat back on his haunches again.

'Max?'

She looked as lost as he felt. Maybe that meant she felt the same way.

He sure as hell hoped so.

Every nerve-end was quivering in desire. He'd raised her to fever pitch—and now he'd stopped?

'This is so not fair,' Cyn whispered. He couldn't do this to her. He couldn't arouse her to the point where her brain was turned to mush and then stop. 'I need you inside me. Now.'

'Are you taking charge?' His eyes glittered. Challenge? Interest? Both?

Ha. She could do that. 'Yeah. I'm taking charge.' She sat up and pushed him backwards. 'Got a problem with that?'

He grinned. 'I thought you were supposed to be quiet and sweet and shy? Cynderella?'

She shook her head. 'I'm Cynthia.'

'Cyn.' The diminutive came out as a hiss of pleasure as she moved to straddle him. His eyes widened. 'Oh, yes.'

Wow. So she could make him feel the way he made her feel? Turn him to mush?

She wriggled. Just a tiny bit. And was rewarded with a soft gasp.

Yeah. She could turn him to mush.

She tilted her hips. Rocked slowly, gently. Forward and back.

'Oh-h-h.' He was quivering. 'Cyn. We… I…'

'Yes?'

'Condom,' he ground out.

She'd been concentrating so hard on blowing his mind, she'd forgotten. 'Where?'

It looked as if he had to make a real effort to think. Good.

'Top drawer,' he said finally.

She leaned over to open the drawer, and blinked when she saw the size of the box. Max Taylor clearly liked sex. And had a lot of it.

Her stomach turned to water.

'Cyn?' He sat up, clearly worried by her silence.

'I'm there,' she whispered. Though her heart felt as if it had just been run over by a steamroller. She'd thought this was special. That he reacted this way just to her. But in the end she was just another notch on his bedpost. Max had been under extreme pressure for the last couple of days, thinking he was about to lose his reputation and his business. Sex was his safety valve.

And she was the nearest available woman.

That was the only reason why he was having sex with her.

If she had any pride, she'd leave right now. Except…this would be the third time they'd slept together. Which, in Max's terms, meant the end of the relationship anyway. Definitely the end, for her—though he'd ruined her for other men. And she wanted to make a memory to last her through the years to come.

Slowly, shakily, she ripped the foil packet open. Rolled the condom over him. Lifted herself up as he lay back, and guided him into her.

'Ah, Cyn.' He shivered and lay back again as she lowered herself over him.

That look on his face. Passion. Intensity. But she knew now it wasn't for her, it was for what they were doing. *I'm *good* at things I love doing.* His work. Cooking. Sex.

She needed to keep in mind that they weren't making love. That this didn't mean the same to him as it did to her. For him, this was just physical. What was the saying? 'In the dark, all cats are grey.' Grey as her business suit.

She forced the tears back. Not now. She'd cry for him later.

But now, she'd concentrate on making love. On saying goodbye to him in her own special way. She rocked against him, taking it slow, letting the pressure build and build and build. Not saying a word, but telling him with her body that she loved him. And she understood that he wasn't for her. And that this was goodbye.

Max reached for her hands, held them tightly. As if he were drowning—just as she was. As her movements grew faster, so the pressure of his fingers against hers increased.

'Cyn. Kiss me,' he whispered. 'Please?'

She leaned down and closed her eyes so he couldn't see her heart breaking. And when she kissed him, she knew that she was kissing him goodbye. Even as her climax rippled through her, tiny ripples of pleasure that bloomed and crashed into each other—even as she sank down to rest her head against his shoulder and felt his arms wrap tightly round her—she knew that it was over.

And somehow she had to find the strength to walk away.

When Max came out of the bathroom, Cyn had retrieved her clothes from the floor and was starting to get dressed. 'Where are you going?' he asked, frowning.

'Home. It's over.'

'What?' His head was spinning. They'd just made love. He knew it had been as good for her as it had been for him. And that it had been more than just good sex. Why was she going?

'It's over,' she repeated. 'The third time we've had sex. I know about your three-dates-and-it's-over rule.'

'What are you talking about?' He marched round to her side of the bed and circled her wrist with his fingers.

She lifted her chin. 'You never date women more than three times. You said yourself, you don't want commitment. You left Gina because you didn't want commitment.'

'I left Gina because we weren't right for each other,' he corrected. 'And this—you and me—this is different.'

'No, it's not.' She sounded weary. 'You're still in the thrill-of-the-chase phase. You'll be bored with me by the end of the week, and I'm not going to put myself through the heartache of losing you when you move on to somebody else.'

'Logically, by walking out, you're losing me,' he pointed out.

'But it's my choice.'

'It's not what I'd choose.' He waited a beat. 'Cyn. Stay.'

She looked close to tears and he ached to pull her into his arms. But then they'd end up having sex again. It'd only be postponing this conversation. And the longer they left it, the more painful it was going to be.

'Why? So we can have sex again?'

Ha. She knew it, too. 'No,' he said softly. 'Because I don't want you to go. And what just happened between us wasn't just sex.'

'Wasn't it?'

Oh, come on. Surely she realised. 'It was making love, Cyn, and you know it.' He lifted his chin and stared at her. 'I… Oh, hell, this doesn't happen to me. I don't chase women.'

She scoffed. 'Right.'

He winced. 'I don't mean that as it sounded. I don't think I'm God's gift to women and that any female who comes within a ten-foot radius of me wants to sleep with me! What I mean is, I'm dedicated to my career. Yes, I date a lot. And I keep things light, not serious. But if a woman says no to me, I can live with it.'

'You don't send her flowers and chocolates to wheedle her back into your bed?'

'No. Only you. And I wasn't trying to wheedle you into my bed.' He wanted her back in his life.

'Well, I'm saying no.'

'I said if *a* woman says no, I can live with it. But you're not just any woman, Cyn.' He blew out a breath. 'This hasn't happened to me before. Ever. The way I feel about you…yeah, it scares me. But it scares me more to think you're going to walk out on me. You're The One. The one I never even realised I was looking for, until I found you. I want to be with you, Cyn. I want to wake up every morning with you in my arms.'

'It's just lust. A passing phase.' She flapped a hand at him. 'Give it a while and you'll be back to running around with your tall, skinny blondes.'

She really thought he'd do what her dad did? Okay. He'd spell it out for her. 'Firstly, I've never cheated on a girlfriend. Ever. Secondly, what I feel for you isn't just lust. That night on the bank of the Thames…' He shook his head. 'I've never, ever done anything like that in public before. You put me in such a whirl, I forget where I am— all I can think about is you. And, thirdly, I don't want a tall, skinny blonde. Want me to show you what I want? What I really, *really* want?' Without waiting for an answer, he tugged at her wrist and pulled her over to the cheval mirror. He stood behind her, one hand wrapped round her waist and his chin resting on her shoulder. 'This is what I want. You.'

Looking at herself naked wasn't something Cyn did. She rarely looked in a mirror, full stop. She certainly didn't study her nude body, and it made her feel uncomfortable.

Max obviously sensed it, because he tightened his hold on her waist. 'You turn me on, Cyn. As I think you can probably feel.'

Er, yes. A certain part of his anatomy was speaking very clearly for him.

'What I see before me is a woman who's very far from ordinary. A woman who's clever and whose mind excites me.'

He wanted her to believe he was interested in her mind, mere minutes after they'd just had hot sex? Oh, please, that was the oldest line in the book.

'And your body excites me just as much,' he whispered. 'The first time I met you, you were wearing a face-pack. A mask. Second time round, you were in another mask— the urban sophisticate. I couldn't see any bare skin from the base of your throat to the tips of your toes—and it made me want to unwrap you and discover who you really were.

Your clothes skimmed your curves, teasing and hinting and driving me crazy. That's why I kissed you in the car. That's why I wouldn't let anyone else dance with you—I wanted you all to myself.'

She was silent.

'Pure and simple, I just wanted you. I connect with you on… Oh, hell, I can't find the right words. In your working clothes, you look who you are—a professional. My equal. And here, right now, in front of me—you're just you. The woman who can turn me on with just one look. The woman I want to be with for the rest of my days. You've no idea how hard I'm trying not to scoop you up in my arms, drag you back to my bed and leap on you. I want to touch you, Cyn. All over. I want to make love to you again. And again and again and again, until we're both sated. Though I don't think I'll ever be able to have enough of you.'

The hand around her waist slid upward, cupped one breast; she watched, almost hypnotised, as his finger and thumb closed around her nipple, and it beaded instantly. 'Your breasts are beautiful.' He let his hand slide over her midriff until it rested on the curve of her hip. 'Here, you're soft and the perfect hourglass shape. And, before you protest, remember I'm an architect. I've told you this before. I know angles and proportions. And I know what I see. I see lovely, luscious curves. Curves that drive me crazy.'

His hand slipped lower, between her legs. 'And here… you're so responsive to my touch. I can't get enough of you.'

'That's just sex,' she said dryly.

'Oh, no.' He nibbled her earlobe. 'It's much, much more than just sex. And, seeing as you're the one who brought it up, I've had enough sex to know the difference.'

Her face flamed. 'Gratitude, then. You were scared as

hell that your business was going down the drain and I helped you find out what was happening.'

'This isn't gratitude, either.' He pulled her closer. 'I'm grateful to you, yes, for fixing my computer and finding out the truth about Helen Jones—but what I feel definitely isn't just gratitude.' He paused. 'Though you're right about one thing. The way I feel about you scares the hell out of me, because it's like nothing else I've ever known. I found myself sketching you right in the middle of a blueprint. You've interrupted my sleep for the last week. Want to know why?'

'Why?' she whispered.

'Because you're the only woman I've met who's ever made me want to put her first.'

'No.' She shook her head, not daring to trust what he was saying. 'It's too soon. Too fast. We barely know each other.'

'I think the technical name for it is *coup de foudre*. When it happens, it happens fast and there's nothing you can do about it. It happened when I found this house. Instant recognition that here was where I wanted to be.' He brushed his lips across the nape of her neck. 'I've known you for, what, two weeks? Three? I dunno.' He shook his head. 'I haven't got a grip on time where you're concerned. Though it's not important. I feel as if I've known you for ever. I know you at a deep level. Where it really matters. You understand me, and I understand you. I've told you things I've never told anyone else, and I think you've shared things like that with me, too.'

Yeah. She had. She'd told him about her dad.

'Prince Charming and Cinderella had their happy ending.' He pressed his cheek against hers and held her gaze in the mirror. 'Why can't we?'

'What are you saying?' That he was Prince Charming?

'I'm saying I want you in my life, Cyn. Permanently.

I'll always be a workaholic, and I don't think I could ever change that, but I'll always make time for you. For our children, if you want babies.'

'Babies?' He was talking about babies? 'Hang on, I'm only twenty-seven.' And there was so much more she wanted to do with her career, first.

'We've got plenty of time. There's no rush.' He smiled. 'But, just so you know, I like the idea of having a little girl. A little brown-eyed girl, just like her mum.'

He wanted to make *babies* with her? This sounded serious. But just how serious was he? 'So if I wanted to move out of London, if I wanted to go and live in the country, you'd agree?' she tested.

'I'd hate it. I'd absolutely hate it.' His eyes glittered with honesty. 'But, yes, I'd do it for you.'

She believed him. 'I don't want to move,' she admitted. 'I like living in London.'

'Come and live with me?'

'Give up my house, you mean?'

He shook his head. 'You don't have to. We could live half the time at your place and half the time at mine. Whatever you like.'

'What about your work?'

He shrugged. 'I can work just as well at your house.'

'What, with just a drawing board and a laptop?'

'I lived and worked here when I didn't even have a full set of floorboards or a proper roof,' he reminded her. 'Cyn, I don't care where I live. Or where I work. As long as I'm with you.'

'But…' she frowned '…you love your house.'

'I know. Like I told you, I fell for it, the first time I saw it. I knew it was the right place for me. But I've discovered that I love you more,' he said simply. 'Last night, when I came home, the house just felt empty. Bricks and mortar. It wasn't enough for me, any more. It didn't feel right, without you in it too. I wanted to drive back over to you, hammer on your door and beg you to come back with me. Or beg you to let me stay with you.'

She took a deep breath. 'I don't know if I'm ready for this.'

'Then we'll wait until you are ready.' His face was very, very serious. And very nervous; was it her imagination, or was he worried that she would turn him down? 'I'll wait for you, however long it takes. I want you with me, Cyn. I want you to be the one I wake up to every morning. I want to fall asleep in your arms at night. I want to share my life with you, through the good times and the bad.' He held her close. 'Let me prove to you how much I love you—and that I'll never, ever let you down.'

Then it finally hit her. Max had said he loved her. He loved her more than his house, more than his job. *He loved her.* And he was ready to make a commitment. To her.

So maybe it was time to take some risks. Because, with Max by her side, they weren't really risks after all. They were possibilities.

'Would you build me an office?' she asked.

'Sure. Where?'

'How about here?'

She actually felt his heartbeat speeding up. 'You're going freelance?'

That was something else she liked about him—he was bright. She didn't have to spell everything out for him. 'Maybe that way, we might get to see a bit of each other. Between work.'

He smiled. 'I used to hate sharing my space. When I was working in a practice, I couldn't wait to have an office all of my own. But these last two days, working with you… You distract me, but I don't want to go back to being on my own. How about instead of me building you an office, I let you rearrange mine? Share it with me?'

He was offering her his heart. His home—yeah, that definitely meant his heart.

Though there was still that tiny, tiny nagging doubt. 'You were engaged before. To Gina. And it didn't work out.'

'Because we were both too young. Because she expected me to put her first. Because we weren't right for each other. With you, it's different. We're both old enough to know what we want out of life. You don't expect me to put you first, but I want to.' His gaze held hers in the mirror. 'That's how I know this is the real thing. That you're The One. I love you, Cyn.'

He loved her.

She couldn't shake the fears. 'But you loved Gina. And you left her.'

'I thought I loved her,' he said honestly. 'And I did. But I didn't love her enough. And, believe me, the way I felt about her is nothing like the way I feel about you. It's like the difference between a flatplan and three-D. Between monochrome and technicolour. Between stereo and mono. With you, it's like having an extra dimension. An extra sense. Something that just isn't there with anyone else.' He took a deep breath. 'I love you. And I want to be with you. Always. That's why I couldn't just leave it when you told me it was over. Why I sent you chocolates and flowers and poetry and music. If—well, if my computer system had been fine on Friday, I would have come over to your office and persuaded you to have lunch with me. And I would have told you how I feel about you. How it's like nothing else I've known—and I don't want a life without you. I need you, Cyn. Without you, I'm not complete.'

He meant it. He really loved her. He'd fallen for her, the way she'd fallen for him. Instantly. 'I've told you things

I've never told anyone else,' she said quietly. 'So maybe it's time to tell you another. I love you.'

A heartbeat passed. Another. And then he spun her round to face him. His mouth found hers—urgently, desperately. 'This is a story you're never going to be able to tell your mum,' he said when he finally broke the kiss. 'Or mine.'

She frowned. 'What?'

He grinned. 'That I proposed to you when we were both stark naked and standing in front of a mirror.'

'You haven't—' she began—and was silenced when Max dropped to one knee and lifted her left hand.

'"Come live with me and be my love,"' he said softly. 'I don't care if the wedding's tomorrow or next year or in a decade or when we're ninety. I just want you to be with me for the rest of our lives. I love you, Cynthia Reynolds. And I need to know… Will you marry me?'

It was too soon. Too fast. Crazy.

And absolutely right.

So there was only one thing she could say. 'Yes.'

EPILOGUE

Eighteen months later

'YOU know you said you might try acting again,' Cyn said to Lisa.

'Yeah.'

'Well, we have a job for you.'

Lisa frowned. 'What sort of job?'

Max casually pulled his wife off the edge of his desk and onto his lap. 'You did a good job of playing fairy godmother, when you introduced us to each other.'

'And when you found Jason a new job,' Cyn added.

'No, that was Max. *He* was the one who gave him a chance to wipe his slate clean,' Lisa said. 'I just typed the letter. And you were the one who got Helen back on the straight and narrow.'

'Splitting hairs.' Cyn waved a dismissive hand. 'Anyway, we have another fairy godmother role for you.'

'Minus the fairy,' Max added.

Lisa blinked. 'You what?'

'Fairy godmother. Minus "fairy". Equals…?' Cyn made frantic small circles with one hand. 'Do the maths, Lise.'

Lisa just stared at her, dumbstruck.

Max sighed. 'I told you that you were being too

oblique, Cyn. Lisa, we want you to be godmother. To our baby.'

There was a two-second pause while it sank in. Then, 'Oh, my God, you're having a baby!' Lisa shrieked.

'Gratifying, isn't it?' Max asked, stroking Cyn's hair and grinning.

'Definitely. This time, she screamed even louder than when we asked her to be bridesmaid,' Cyn responded, laughing.

'I'm going to be a godmother. *I'm going to be a god-mother!*' Lisa yelled.

Max handed her the phone, adding in a stage whisper to Cyn, 'I think our secretary might have some personal calls to make…'

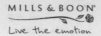

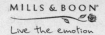

MILLS & BOON®   0406/01b

Live the emotion

Modern
romance™

BOUGHT FOR THE MARRIAGE BED
by Melanie Milburne

Nina will do anything to keep her twin's baby from harm.
So when Marc Marcello wants to take his brother's child,
Nina lets herself be bought as Marc's bride instead. But
what price can be placed on her…in his bed?

THE ITALIAN'S WEDDING ULTIMATUM
by Kim Lawrence

Alessandro Di Livio always protects his family, even
seducing gold digging Sam Maguire to keep her away from
his brother-in-law! But when passion leads to pregnancy,
Alessandro wants to keep Sam as his wife – and their baby
as his heir!

THE INNOCENT VIRGIN by Carole Mortimer

Abby Freeman is thrilled when she gets a job as a TV chat
show host, and who better to grill than famous journalist
Max Harding? Max is happy to let Abby get close – but
only in private. How can Abby get the story…without
losing her innocence?

RUTHLESS REUNION by Elizabeth Power

Sanchia has amnesia but when Alex Sabre recognises her,
she realises they once knew each other intimately. To
unlock her past Sanchia must spend time with Alex. What
happens when she learns the truth about the man she's
falling in love with…again?

On sale 5th May 2006

*Available at WHSmith, Tesco, ASDA, Borders, Eason,
Sainsbury's and most bookshops*

www.millsandboon.co.uk

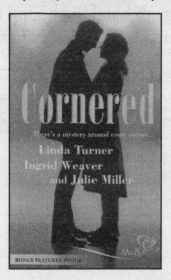

Part basset, part beagle, all Cupid... can a matchmaking hound fetch a new love for his owner?

For Nina Askew, turning forty means freedom – from the ex-husband, from their stuffy suburban home. Freedom to have her own apartment in the city, freedom to focus on what *she* wants for a change. And what she wants is a bouncy puppy to cheer her up. Instead she gets...Fred.

Overweight, smelly and obviously suffering from some kind of doggy depression, Fred is light-years from perky. But for all his faults, he does manage to put Nina face-to-face with Alex Moore, her gorgeous younger neighbour...

On sale 5th May 2006
Don't miss out!

Available at WHSmith, Tesco, ASDA, Borders, Eason, Sainsbury's and all good paperback bookshops

www.millsandboon.co.uk